CW00340652

LAMBERT & BUTLER'S CIGARETTES

AMBROSE

LAMBERT & BUTLER'S CIGARETTES

BILLY COTTON

LAMBERT & BUTLER'S CIGARETTES

DUKE ELLINGTON

LAMBERT & BUTLER'S CIGARETTES

ROY FOX

LAMBERT & BUTLER'S CIGARETTES

JACK HYLTON

LAMBERT & BUTLER'S CIGARETTES

JACK JACKSON

LAMBERT & BUTLER'S CIGARETTES

CHARLIE KUNZ

LAMBERT & BUTLER'S CIG

SYDNEY KYTE

LAMBERT & BUTLER'S CIGARETTES

JACK PAYNE

LAMBERT & BUTLER'S CIGARETTES

LOU PREAGER

LAMBERT & BUTLER'S CIGARETTES

HARRY ROY

LAMBERT & BUTLER'S CIG

DEBROY SOMERS

GERALDO

CARROLL GIBBONS

NAT GONELLA

HENRY HALL

RIAN LAWRANCE

SYD. LIPTON

JOE LOSS

RAY NOBLE

LEW STONE

RUDY VALLEE

PAUL WHITEMAN

MAURICE WINNICK

And the bands played on

Sid Colin

ELM TREE BOOKS
Hamish Hamilton · London

to Dena

who thought she was marrying a musician,
and got stuck with a writer.

First published in Great Britain 1977
by Elm Tree Books/Hamish Hamilton Ltd
Garden House 57–59 Long Acre London WC2E 9JZ
First published in this edition 1980

Copyright © 1977 by Sid Colin

ISBN 0 241 10448 3

Typeset by Filmtype Services Limited, Scarborough
Printed Photolitho in Great Britain by Ebenezer Baylis & Son Ltd.
The Trinity Press, Worcester, and London

Contents

Acknowledgements

I am indebted to many authors and their works for information about people and places which make an appearance in this book. Among them are: *The Dance Band Era* by Albert McCarthy (Studio Vista, 1971), *British Dance Bands* by Brian Rust and Edward S. Walker (Storyville, 1973), *After the Ball* by Ian Whitcomb (Allan Lane, 1972), *The Big Bands* by George T. Simon (Macmillan, 1971), and *The Twenties* by Alan Jenkins (Heinemann, 1974). A special note of appreciation to Dave Shand for his Jack Hylton stories, and to other musician friends, notably Harry Hayes and Jack Bentley, for jogging my memory. And thanks, too, to Brian Vincent for compiling the select discography.

Finally, I am indebted to the following for permission to reproduce the photographs in this volume: Mrs Kenneth Bird, British Broadcasting Corporation, British Film Institute, *Dancing Times*, Decca Records, Fairfield Halls, Angelo Hornak, Imperial War Museum, Max Jones Collection, Doug Le Vicki, Keystone Press Agency, Mander and Mitchenson Theatre Collection, *Melody Maker*, Herbert R. Parkins, Pathé/EMI, Popperfoto, Radio Times Hulton Picture Library, Brian Rust, Savoy Hotel, and Syndication International. Every effort has been made to trace the copyright holders of the photographs; however, should there be any omission in this respect, the appropriate acknowledgements will gladly be made in future editions.

Foreword

AT THIS STAGE OF THE GAME, AND ON looking back, I don't think that I could envisage a more varied or exciting existence than that of being associated with the musical profession, with its complement of extrovert characters, talented and otherwise. Many of the situations in which I found myself involved were pleasurable, some almost unbelievable, and I could well understand the incredulous attitude of the man in the street on being told a few of the seemingly impossible stories about musicians. It was, therefore, with no surprise whatsoever, no difficulty, and certainly much pleasure that I found myself identifying with this book by Sid Colin.

I was cheered, saddened, and in much sympathy with it throughout, and when I say that I shared with the author much of the action described, you can well imagine my enjoyment on being taken back through the years – years in which I was enriched through getting to know so many great people in a profession to which I am grateful to belong. The 'relationships' between the bandleaders and the musicians, between the West End dancing customer and the 'unapproachable' Maestro d'Orchestra; the postures of the various film producers, television pro-ducers and managers towards musicians in general; the demand for bland tunes which were easy to dance to against the musicians' desire to improvise or play a little jazz – these were the circumstances in which our professional lives were played out, and which the author evokes so well.

One of the many important functional sections of the musical profession is that of the jazz musician, a creative animal in his own specialised field. The jazzman tended to find that his particular talents appealed in the beginning to minimal audiences, and his monetary rewards reflected this. The meagre pittance he received was further endangered by the association by the 'sensational' Press of jazz and the upsurge of crime at the time that that music was growing; unfortunately, some of the murder, rape and drug offences took place on premises in which jazz groups were employed, a fact much played upon by that section of the media. Consequently when the word 'jazz' was accepted into the vocabulary of the man in the street it became, through these irrational and exaggerated reports, synonomous with those very offences. It was a sorry state, and wholly unwarranted. The position today, I'm happy to say, is very much better.

I've had the pleasure of working with Sid Colin through the years of the Ambrose Orchestra, the Heralds of Swing, the Squadronaires RAF Dance Orchestra and countless freelance jazz sessions – years when the often maligned musician was simply trying to do his job – produce good music – as best he knew how. Sid's book goes a long way towards setting the record straight.

GEORGE CHISHOLM

Introduction: *The boys in the band*

A POTENT MEMORY OF MY OBSESSION
with dance music is filling the back pages of my Latin notebook with
drawings of bands. These bands were immense; fantastic orchestras of
unbelievable grandeur. There were row upon serried row of violinists,
whole banks of trumpet players, galaxies of assorted saxophones, banjoists, sousaphone players, drummers, tympanists, tubular bell ringers,
glockenspielers, marimbaphonists; one page of a school exercise book was
too small to accommodate them – they demanded, and got, the full double
spread. Only later did I discover that the myriad violinists, banjoists and
guitarists I had drawn with such loving care and in such meticulous detail
were all playing their instruments left-handed. Think of it! Page after page
of Paul McCartneys! It may well be the reason why I never came fully to
appreciate the art of the Beatles.

At school, jazz filled my days, my evenings and my nights, drowning
out everything else. Weekdays were spent daydreaming (and drawing
bands), evenings were spent hunched over the guitar and the Eddie Lang
Original Barré System Guitar Method (in spite of my left-handedness, I
did learn to play the instrument the right way round). Saturdays were
devoted to the long bus ride to Levy's Record Shop in the East End, there
to discover what treasures had newly arrived from the States. Records by

Red Nichols, The Harlem Footwarmers, McKinney's Cotton Pickers, Louis Armstrong. Even the brand names on the labels had a special magic: Victor, Okeh, Bluebird.

By the age of fifteen, the jazz bug had well and truly bitten, and as anyone will tell you, it carries a malaise for which there is no known cure. And so, when I announced to my family that I intended giving up what was an already hopelessly blighted academic career in order to go on tour with a band, they received the news with stoical resignation. A junkie in the family!

What I remember most vividly about my life as a dance band musician in the West End, in clubs, in restaurants, in big bands and small bands, is laughing a lot. It most certainly wasn't so, but looking back it seems to me now that musicians were always laughing at something. At anything. At nothing? At bandleaders: Ambrose's fiddle playing, Maurice Winnick's conducting, Geraldo's cockney accent, Lew Stone's accident-proneness (he was for ever falling off the front of the bandstand). At customers: the way they danced, the way they looked. At other musicians: the corny ones; those who thought they knew how to play modern dance music, but didn't; music hall pit orchestras; German dance bands. Musicians even laughed at the things they most admired; if Louis or Duke did something miraculous on a gramophone record, the response was always laughter. Delighted, ecstatic laughter.

Yet how could there have been so much laughter when musicians were treated the way they were? Bullied by bandleaders, cheated by their managers, insulted by *maîtres d'hôtel,* they were avoided by practically everybody else. Socially they were far beyond the pale; I can remember few parents who, threatened with a musician as a suitor, did not lock up their silverware and commit their daughters to the care of nuns. In television studios, too, where I have spent a good deal of my life since I stopped playing, the arrival of musicians is usually greeted with something less than enthusiasm: 'Oh God, here comes the band.' It is as if the studio were about to be invaded by the combined forces of Attila the Hun and the Los Angeles chapter of Hell's Angels.

After the war I was undecided about what to do with my life. For big bands there seemed to be no alternative but to tour, and I had had enough of that with the Squadronaires. Besides, I wanted to get married, and I did not see myself in the role of the Flying Dutchman nor my future wife as Mother Courage. But what was even more alarming was what was happening to the guitar. It was being electrified! That noble instrument, which had graced the knee of Andrès Segovia and Freddie Green alike, was now attached to a sinister looking black box by an obscene umbilical cord, and when struck would emit such a wailing and a screeching as might rise from the pit of damnation itself. The idea that I would have to learn to plug myself in and twiddle little black knobs before my instrument would utter a sound threw me into total panic.

Then, one day early in 1946, I was at the BBC's Aeolian Hall in Bond Street for a band session. I was in the control booth with the producer, who was expressing dissatisfaction with the orchestral balance in the studio. Flicking his talk-back switch he demanded that somebody on the band rostrum move the stand mike a few inches. A guitarist, who was a stranger to me but was one of the new amplified breed, volunteered his services, and with his electric guitar in one hand, he grasped the stand mike firmly with the other. At which point, he assumed an expression of mild surprise, and the kind of pose that children strike when they are playing a game called Statues. After a few moments, the producer requested that he, the electric guitarist, stop fooling about and get on with what he was supposed to be doing. The guitarist continued to play Statues. Only then did it occur to somebody else that perhaps all was not well. Master switches were hastily thrown, the studio was plunged into darkness, and the unfortunate guitarist collapsed into an untidy and quite unconscious heap on the floor. It was at that precise moment that I decided that the dance music profession would just have to get along as best it could without me.

It will not escape the notice of the reader that my version of the history of dance music is somewhat biased in favour of the rank and file musicians – the 'side men' as the Americans call them. I make no apology for that. I had the pleasure of their company for many years, and it seems to me now that I have liked no one nearly as much as I liked the boys in the band. They were a good group and I salute them.

Here is Sid Colin, well-known young guitarist-vocalist, who is going to the Cafe de Paris with Lew Stone. He is also very busy turning out material—songs and patter—for various cabaret artists, and is writing the script for Sid Millward's next radio session, on Oct. 11.

11

The night and the music

THE TIME IS HALF PAST MIDNIGHT.
Under a warm golden light, the band sits aloof on its nine-inch throne, dispensing the most expensive dance music in Europe. 'I get too hungry for dinner at eight, I like the theatre but never come late . . .' The music rolls around the floor like silver pennies. '. . . That's why the lady is a tramp.'

The bandleader, immaculate in his suit of tails and a shirt-front so white it could bring on a mild attack of snow blindness, regards the dancers with an expression both benign and sardonic, master of all he surveys. He directs the orchestra with gestures no more demonstrative than those of an antique dealer bidding for a Sheraton sideboard at Christie's, but the pianist modulates adroitly and the brass section, screwing in their harmon mutes, respond to a man. 'The way you wear your hat, the way you sip your tea, the mem'ry of all that, no, no, they can't take that away from me.'

The dancers, undulating on a floor no larger than a dentist's waiting room, shuffle aimlessly, claim a vacant square foot of space from their neighbours and avoid bodily contact with the skill of Japanese commuters. A ground bass of animated small talk rises on the richly scented air, accented at odd moments by the shrill cries of women with pitiless upper-class voices. They are a dressy crowd; the men dinner-jacketed or

And the bands played on

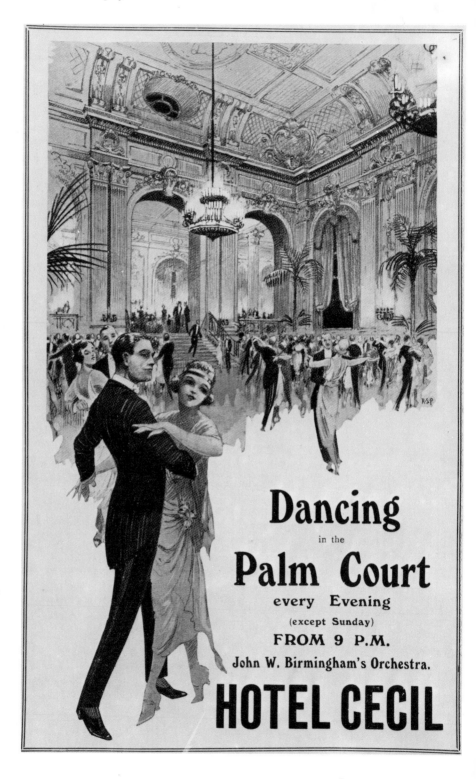

The night and the music in 1922. The artist has let himself go here; The Hotel Cecil was surely less like the Palace of Versailles than this

tail-suited, the women glittering in their ankle-length gowns. They shuffle past the bandstand, smiling relentlessly and hoping for some sign of recognition from the maestro. 'Good evening, Mr Ambrose.' A nod in reply will anoint you a man about town, a sad smile as one of the élite.

One such is favoured with a handshake, into which he sandwiches a white five-pound note. 'Could we possible have a rhumba?' Ambrose acknowledges that there is indeed such a possibility. Another dancer, some yokel who knows no better, tries the same gambit with a pound, and is rewarded by having the offending note stuffed contemptuously into his top pocket as he passes. Pound notes are for taxi drivers and cloakroom ladies, not for celebrated bandleaders with expensive tastes.

That was the Café de Paris in 1937, and all over the West End of London in that vintage year, the bands were playing on. Outside, the chill winds of depression might be blowing, Spaniards might be locked in a savage civil war, the Japanese might be taking Shanghai and Peking, and the Nazis might be plotting to annex Austria and the Sudetenland. But in the restaurants of the great London hotels and in the exclusive supper clubs, the rich and the famous, the well-heeled and the well-beloved, were dancing the nights away.

The Savoy Hotel it was, in 1922 or thereabouts, which presented the West Enders with their first recognisable dance band. Until then, bands had been a raggle taggle of assorted instruments – cornet, trombone, soprano saxophone, piano, banjo and drums – the players slavishly imitating the sounds they had first heard when The Original Dixieland Jazz Band crossed the Atlantic in 1919 and astounded the natives assembled at the London Hippodrome and the Hammersmith Palais with their raucous, undisciplined, mostly improvised music. To ears unfamiliar with the real McCoy, it passed for jazz.

But by 1923, bands were taking on a new look. Seven or eight dinner-jacketed gents, slick haired and well scrubbed, presented themselves in an orderly row across the front of the bandstand; to one side, the saxophone section, two altos and a tenor; to the other, the brass, two trumpets and a trombone. A fiddle player or two, and a crooner nursing his megaphone like a beached Varsity coxswain completed this number. Behind them, one step up, were the drummer, the pianist, the sousaphone player and the banjoist. Front and centre, smiling urbanely, groomed and polished, dressed as for a royal banquet, stood the bandleader, sometimes cradling a violin in the crook of his arm, sometimes wielding a baton the length of a rapier. And before each of his musicians there stood a music stand, its metal struts tastefully hidden from view by a velvet banner proclaiming the name of the band. Music stands, for goodness sake! These guys could actually read music! Or so they seemed to claim.

The West End in the 'twenties. Top left, Ray Starita and his Ambassadors Club Band (his brother Rudy is on drums); bottom left, Teddy Brown and his Band posing in front of the famous double staircase at the Café de Paris; and, above, Debroy Somers conducting the Orpheans at the Savoy

That wild and woolly Yankee music had been tamed and domesticated; it had been disciplined and deodorized and forced into respectability, rendered suitable for the ears of kings and princes, for the dancing feet of duchesses and débutantes. At the Savoy, Debroy Summers, a charmer with dark wavy hair and a Pepsodent smile, was leading the Savoy Orpheans. A young violinist named Bert Ambrose was establishing himself at the Embassy, an exclusive supper club in Old Bond Street, much frequented by the Prince of Wales and his cronies.

By 1925, dance music was being played all over town. Jack Payne was at the Hotel Cecil in the Strand, Ben Davis at the Carlton in the Haymarket. Ray Starita had a band at the Piccadilly, while his brother Al was opening the brand new Kit Cat Club on the other side of the Circus.

It was in the 'thirties that dance music, smooth, sophisticated and sure of itself, came to full flowering in London's grand hotels and supper clubs. The banjo and the sousaphone had been renounced in favour of the Spanish guitar and the string bass, instruments more suited to the insouciance of the slick popular songs from Broadway and the talking pictures. But apart from that, the look of the bandstand had scarcely changed.

Saxophonists selected their reeds as as much care as fly fishermen their flies. Either that, or this is a little-known Chinese card game

The music went around and around, and so did the musicians. Ambrose at the Mayfair, Harry Roy at the Café Anglais, Jack Jackson at the Dorchester and Sydney Lipton at Grosvenor House. Maurice Winnick at the San Marco, Carroll Gibbons at the Savoy, Jack Harris at Ciro's.

In 1931, a quiet American with a cat-like smile, whose name was Roy Fox and who could wear a Hawes and Curtis tail suit the way most Englishmen only wished they could, formed a band to open a plush room in Jermyn Street called the Monseigneur. In October 1932, that same band was taken over by a pianist-arranger with a passion for football, and the name Lew Stone was added to the list of favourite bandleaders.

And so it went on; the bands played, the dancers danced, the scent of Romeo y Julieta curled up to the ceiling and mingled with the Mitsouko under the warm golden light. Head waiters discreetly steered celebrities to the tables closest to the dance floor, and nonentities to the draughty corners next to the swinging kitchen doors. All was right with the world. Until one night in March 1941, when a German bomb landed neatly on the floor of the Café de Paris and killed a young bandleader from British Guiana whose name was Ken Johnson and who was called Snakehips because of the sinuous grace of his body. The West End was never the same again.

It should not be thought that the music their admirers will always associate with such famous bands as Ambrose, Lew Stone and Jack Jackson, resembles in the very least what was played nightly at the Mayfair, the Monseigneur and the Dorchester. Those elaborate orchestrations of popular tunes of the day were reserved exclusively for broadcasting and recording. What the patrons of the West End hotels and supper clubs demanded and got was soft lights and sweet music for dancing; the brass tightly bottled up, the rhythm section dainty and discreet, the saxophones polite, and all delivering an unbroken daisy chain of thirty-two-bar choruses in two tempi, quickstep and foxtrot. At any moment of their choice, say between the turtle soup and the sole meunière, the dancers might take to the floor, hop around for a minute or two, and never suffer the embarrassment of being caught in mid-hop when the music stopped.

The prime ingredient on this conveyor belt pot-pourri was the 'show tunes'; the hits from Broadway musical comedies, past and present, and more often than not the work of the great songwriters of the 'twenties and 'thirties, Cole Porter, George Gershwin, Rodgers and Hart and Jerome Kern. Not for the smart set the hit-parade fodder of the Palais de Danse. These were globetrotting chaps who knew their New York, may actually have been there in 1938 when Mary Martin stopped the show with 'My Heart Belongs To Daddy', and needed to impress their dancing partners by singing into their ears some garbled version of the lyric. So that is what the bands played, from nine o'clock nightly, oom ching, oom ching, tunes without end, until two o'clock in the morning.

And the bands played on

In the mid-'thirties, when the rhythms of Latin America became popular, the band might be relieved during the evening by a group of musicians wearing frilly shirts, who scraped gourds, clicked claves, shook maracas, bashed bongoes, uttered occasional 'olés' and 'arribas', and could manage the difficult feat of looking madly gay and thoroughly fed up at one and the same time. Such interludes apart, the night and the music belonged to the dance band.

And how did they feel about it, these musicians? Remembering that they were the finest in the land; experts, virtuosi even, to a man? In a word, they were bored. Oom ching, oom ching, all night long. There was music on the music stands but it was rarely referred to. They all knew 'the book' by heart, had long since squeezed from it every mite of musical interest. In the musicians' own parlance, it was a drag.

The dancing customers were no help. All they ever were was a kind of moving wallpaper, to be tolerated or wearily ignored. A chinless wonder clutching his willowy partner arrives in front of the bandstand and catches the bandleader's eye. 'I say,' says he, 'what about playing "You Are The One"?' ' "You Are The One"?' puzzles the bandleader. 'I don't believe I know that.' 'Of course you do,' insists the dancer. 'It goes like this: Night and day – you are the one.'

The West End in the 'thirties. Top left, Maurice Winnick and his Band at the San Marco Restaurant; bottom left, Roy Fox at the Monseigneur; and, below, Geraldo and his Gaucho Tango Orchestra on the roof of the Savoy

CARRIED AWAY

By H. M. BATEMAN

To the general rule that all customers were unworthy of their notice, the musicians observed but one exception: a pretty girl. Not only was she like a melody, she was the only thing that kept them going through the interminable hours of perpetual oom ching. Jackie Hunter, the drummer with Jack Jackson at the Dorchester, perfected a code for alerting the rest of the band to the presence in their midst of one of these rare creatures. From his vantage point aloft at the back of the stand, he would scan the room in search of a beauty; or rather, not to mince matters, a pair of beauties. Having spotted his quarry, he would pass on the information to his colleagues in the following manner: for your run-of-the-mill smasher, a side drum roll. For the girl with the daring cleavage, a drum roll and a cymbal crash. For the main event of the evening, the girl with the truly spectacular superstructure, the roll, the cymbal crash and an urgent four in the bar thumping on the bass drum foot pedal. Only the last was sufficient to arouse the band's interest and lead to a radar-like scanning of the dance floor until all eyes had alighted upon Jackie's prime choice, and had rested there for a brief moment of sincere and heartfelt appreciation.

Another source of endless fun and entertainment was the latest skirmish in a never-ending feud between the musicians and the waiters. No love was ever lost between these two groups, and no opportunity for

These well-dressed revellers were photographed at the Monseigneur in 1933. As you see, they were having a ball

inflicting pain or causing acute embarrassment was ever missed. Once, at the Café de Paris, some dimwitted waiter made the mistake of parking the caviar trolley in a position alongside the bandstand. It wasn't long before every musician had armed himself with a slice of melba toast tucked unobtrusively into the top pocket of his dinner jacket. At the end of each session, as they all passed the trolley en route to the bandroom, they scooped up a goodly portion of the finest Beluga on to the toast and continued onward to their well-earned fifteen-minute break. And what could be a nicer accompaniment to a cool glass of Pilsner than caviar on melba toast? You may imagine the resulting fracas when the band's depredations were uncovered.

Of course, one speaks here of the musicians, the boys in the bands, and not the bandleaders. They were, it must clearly be understood, another tin of caviar altogether. The bandleaders were a race apart, of a status equalled only by that other exotic breed, the *maîtres d'hôtel*. When they were not table hopping, exchanging pleasantries with the customers and sharing their Dom Perignon, their function on the bandstand was, as often as not, merely decorative.

Below, Carroll Gibbons and the Savoy Hotel Orpheans in full fig; right, Jack Jackson looking every inch a bandleader

CARROLL GIBBONS AND THE SAVOY HOTEL ORPHEANS

Romano's Restaurant in the Strand in 1932. The chap in the ungainly position in front of the bandstand is the cabaret and not an unruly customer

However, it was the fashionable thing in the 'twenties and 'thirties for the bandleader to present himself as a musician among musicians. Most of them held a musical instrument, and some of them occasionally played it. Most numerous were the violinist leaders: Ambrose, Sydney Lipton, Jack Harris, Maurice Winnick. There were pianist leaders: Carroll Gibbons, Fred Elizalde; alto saxophone leaders: Howard Jacobs, Ben Davis; trumpeting leaders: Roy Fox and Jack Jackson. And Harry Roy led his band with a clarinet, which while it delighted the paying guests at the Café Anglais, was known to sadden the members of the band and to make their eyes water.

All the same it would be wrong to leave the impression that the relationship between the bandleader and his band was never better than one of mutual distaste. Like many another boss-worker relationship it was a good deal more complex than that. Some bandleaders were fun to work for, some commanded respect, others were heartily loathed.

And of course, these big time musicians were an entirely new breed, and by no means easy to handle. They were immensely skilled, highly paid and fiercely independent. To be playing in any of those West End bands meant that they had reached the pinnacle of their profession. And they knew it. The stars among them moved easily and often from job to job. They were wooed and bid for by rival bandleaders like first-division soccer players. You pushed them around at your peril. Head waiters and restaurant managers were baffled by them. In the feudal hierarchy of their own profession musicians could not be placed. They could not be cowed like waiters, nor kowtowed to like customers, although customers is what they often behaved as if they were. When they finished work at 2.00 a.m. they didn't run for the all-night bus, but leapt into their Aston Martins and their Ford V8's and zoomed off to their mock-Tudor homes in the Stockbroker Belt, to their interior sprung mattresses and their golfing Sundays.

The battle for status was fought nightly in a hundred different hotels and restaurants all over the West End. At the Café de Paris, the band was ordered not to use the customers' entrance in Coventry Street but to confine itself to the kitchen entrance around the corner in Rupert Street. One band defied the order and was promptly fired. A saxophone player (who shall here be nameless) took his revenge by arriving for his last night's work with an empty baritone sax case which he proceeded to fill with the Café's choicest glasswear. They were goblets, beautifully engraved with the initials 'C de P', and so large was his haul that the guilty saxophonist seriously considered changing his name to Charlie de Puyster.

If there ever was a golden age of the dance bands, as we are often asked to believe, then it surely was those years between 1930 and 1939, when the West End thrived and prospered, the bandleaders were superstars, the musicians got paid every Friday night, and it seemed that the good times would never end.

There's something in the air

AT APPROXIMATELY TWENTY-SIX
minutes past ten, the music stops. As the dancers return to their tables, a
hushed expectancy falls upon the room. A cheerful man with a toothbrush
moustache hops nimbly on to the bandstand and fiddles about with the
microphones strategically mounted there. He confides into one of them:
'Testing, testing. One, two, three, four. Peter Piper picked a peck of
pickled peppercorns.' The musicians hunch over their music stands and
leaf through pages of manuscript, checking the running order. The pianist
strikes an 'A', and they tune to it, furtively, like Commandos preparing an
attack. The bandleader raises his arms as if to offer them a benediction
before the battle. At his side, a five-watt light bulb mounted on a stand
glows red, and the band launches itself into the opening bars of its
signature tune.

The bandleader flaps his arms wildly, exhorting a *diminuendo*, and a
dinner-jacketed gent addresses the stand microphone. 'This,' he tells it, 'is
the BBC from London. Dance music until midnight comes to you from the
Dorchester Hotel in the heart of the West End, and is played for you by
Jack Jackson and his Orchestra. They begin their programme with a
brand new arrangement of an old favourite, "Limehouse Blues".'

The brass section raise their unmuted horns and blow with the joyful

Above, Jack Jackson blowing
up a storm; far right, Alvin
Keech, inventor of the
banjulele, shows a lady how
to accompany dance music
on the radio. She looks as if
she expects the loudspeaker
to fight back

It's a Clippertone
The great Rotary Quick-Change Trumpet

Handle it—place it to your lips—play it—
discover for yourself its light responsive action.
What brilliant staccato—and how softly it
blends!

You must sense the superiority of the Clippertone Trumpet by its purity of tone, perfect
tuning and beauty of design.

For a small deposit in cash this trumpet can be
yours, the balance being payable out of income
in twelve small monthly payments.

May we send you particulars!

HAWKES and SON
Denman Street,
Piccadilly Circus, London, W.1

*Acknowledged by
leading artists to
be the finest
instrument on the
market today*

*They
are proud to c
the Clipperto*
H. Thompson
lady Be Good to fo
A. Wilson
Alfredos Orch
J. Raine
Jack Hylons Ba
H. Wild
Savoy Orph
& other leading an

abandon of fat ladies who have just removed their corsets; the drummer discards his discreet wire brushes and attacks his kit with gusto. For the next hour and a half, the diners and the dancers in the restaurant of the Dorchester Hotel will be totally ignored. The band is playing for others, several million of them, gathered around their wireless sets in towns and villages all over the land, and eavesdropping on their music. The band is on the air. The joint is being bugged!

Not that the patrons haven't been warned. At the Mayfair Hotel on Saturday nights, a small white card, not unlike a wedding invitation, would appear on the tables. It read:

> Ambrose and his orchestra are
> broadcasting tonight, and,
> therefore, the band is playing
> considerably louder than usual.

They might reasonably have added, in small italicized type: 'The management does not enjoy this ghastly, ear-splitting noise any more than you do.'

It had all started back in 1923, when the British Broadcasting Company, established the previous year at Savoy Hill, first began to include dance music in its programme of entertainment. A bandleader named Marius B. Winter broadcast from the studio, and from the Carlton Hotel alto saxophone player Ben Davis sent the music of his band floating over the air waves. Around the town, strange creatures, wearing headphones and the expressions latterly reserved for the characters in science fiction movies, were crouched over their primitive receivers, applying cat's whisker to crystal in an often vain attempt to separate the sounds of music from the *Walpurgisnacht* of static which surrounded it.

By 1925 those slapstick pioneering days were already over and broadcasting was nationwide. Wireless sets, stuffed with glowing valves, were available to all, and the sounds which issued from their elaborately fretted loudspeakers, albeit tinny at the top and apt to rattle and buzz like loose bedsprings in the lower register, were beginning to render a reasonable account of the music being transmitted.

The following year, Jack Payne was on the air from the Hotel Cecil, and the newly-born British Broadcasting Corporation could boast its own combo – the London Radio Dance Band led by Sidney Firman. There were one million licence holders.

In 1929, Ambrose was broadcasting regularly from the Mayfair and Fred Elizalde from the Savoy. Jack Payne had taken up residence as leader of the BBC Dance Orchestra, and there were ten million pairs of ears at the receiving end.

'Roll up the carpet and dance', exhorted the BBC announcer in his calm and cultured Reith-approved tones; and up and down the country the obedient listeners responded. They foxtrotted, quickstepped, tangoed and waltzed around their parlours, lounges and living rooms, to music that had hitherto been the exclusive property of the affluent crowd who could afford a night out 'up West'. They chose their favourite among the bandleaders and wrote him letters requesting tunes and pleading for photos and autographs. And this happy chosen few, the maestros lucky enough to have been granted a slice of the air-time cake, were fast becoming rich and famous.

Ambrose and his Band at the Mayfair in 1932. The cartoon is by Fougasse

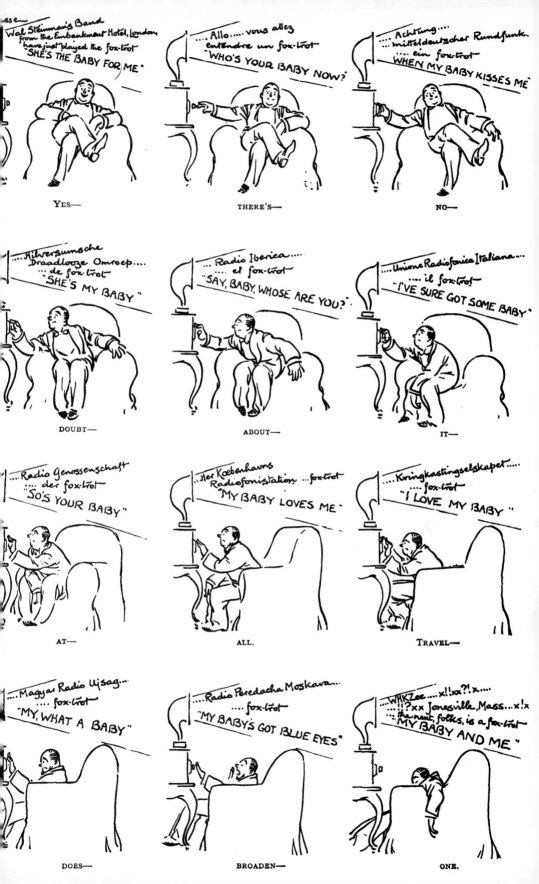

Billy Cotton and his Band in the 'thirties

By 1933, a pattern of late-night dance music (so called) had clearly emerged. Monday through Friday, from ten-thirty until midnight, you could hear, at the flip of a switch, Sydney Lipton from the Grosvenor House, Jack Jackson from the Dorchester, Carroll Gibbons from the Savoy, and Lew Stone from the Monseigneur. And on Saturday nights, the most glittering prize the air waves could afford – Ambrose and his Orchestra from the Mayfair. Dance music every night of the week. But never, it should be added, on Sunday. Not during John Reith's puritanical reign as Director General of the Corporation.

There was more dance music to be found on the air at other times. Lots more. There was lunch-time dance music, tea-time dance music, any-old-time-at-all dance music (oh how we danced in those between-the-wars years). And supplying much of this, or most of it (some said he was outrageously hogging it) was Henry Hall, newly appointed leader of a brand new BBC Dance Orchestra.

From the radio feast being shared by those mentioned, a few crumbs did arrive on the tables of others. From the Dance Palaces at Hammersmith, Streatham, and the Astoria, Charing Cross Road, came the music of Oscar Rabin and his Romany Band, Joe Loss, Lou Preager and Billy Cotton; from the Piccadilly Hotel, Sidney Kyte; from the Café de Paris, Jack Harris, and from Ciro's Club, Maurice Winnick. Jack Hylton and Jack Payne presented their monster showbands whenever they orbited close enough to a microphone to do so, and the rhumba and tango freaks were catered for by Geraldo (who later went straight and formed a first-class dance band), and Mantovani, who was to become king of the swooning swooping strings and one of the few British bandleaders to make a dent in the American record market.

But it was the late-night sessions that were at the heart of the matter,

**Sydney Kyte broadcasting
from the Piccadilly Hotel,
and a frieze of bandleaders
by the cartoonist Sherriffs**

*e (left to right): Maurice Winnick, Billy Cotton, Jack Jackson, Sydney Lipton, Lloyd Shakespeare, Marius B. Winter, Nat Gonella, Joe Loss, Lou Preager
w (left to right): Ambrose, Sidney Kyte, Jack Hylton, Carroll Gibbons, Roy Fox, Lew Stone, Herman Darewski, Harry Roy, Charlie Kunz, Geraldo*

35

and that precious air time was fiercely haggled over and fought for. And why not? For bandleaders it was as vital to their continued well-being as tomorrow's fix was to a junkie.

The BBC, through its ironclad monopoly as the sole purveyor of all this music (there were, in the 'thirties, two commercial stations, Radio Luxembourg and Radio Normandy, but they were without value in this respect), appeared to some bandleaders as a benevolent despot, and to others as a hard-faced tyrant, depending on whether or not you thought you were copping your fair share of the goodies.

One kind of music was conspicuously absent from the BBC schedules, and that was jazz. As far as the Corporation was concerned, jazz was a nasty, noisy, alien nuisance, and they would have none of it. Apart from that, and given that most of the radio producers, heads of departments and administrators who inhabited that stranded liner of a building in Portland Place could not tell a good dance band from a barber shop quartet, the best of the bands actually did get on the air.

Sydney Lipton. He had been the violinist with Billy Cotton's Band, strict tempoing at the Hammersmith Palais, and gypsying around the provincial music hall. But no vestige of that raggle-taggle heritage was apparent when he formed a band in 1932 and took up residence at the Grosvenor House in Park Lane. Tall and dark, he bore himself with the dignity of a Black Rod, and provided dance music which was neat, discreet, and just a trifle dull.

Carroll Gibbons. He was a Massachussetts Yankee with a lazy drawl

Sydney Lipton (left) rehearsing with Al Bowlly in 1938

Carroll Gibbons and the Savoy Orpheans. Paul Fenhoulet (standing, fourth from left) later led the Skyrockets, one of the best of the Services bands

that enveloped the listener like warm molasses. He built his band around his piano playing, which was as warm and witty as he was himself. The band played Savoy music, rich sounds for a world of riches.

Jack Jackson, the Peter Pan of the band world. At the age of thirty, he looked twenty; at forty and fifty, he still looked twenty. Jackson was that rarest of cats, the bandleader who could actually play something. He had been lead trumpet with Jack Hylton in the 'twenties, and later, with Jack Payne, he had blown up the storm which had provided what little taste there was in what otherwise had been the purest porridge. Sadly, when he took his band to the Dorchester in 1933, the trumpet playing took second place to the personality peddling that went with the job. He was fun-loving and lazy, and playing the trumpet was hard graft and who needed it? He even had, attached to the third valve of his horn, a little loop of string, because the valve spring was broken and he could not be bothered to get it fixed.

Lew Stone. When Roy Fox, stricken by ill-health, took himself off to Switzerland, he left his band in the care of his pianist-arranger. It wasn't long before radio dance-band fanciers had acquired a new favourite – Lew Stone and his Monseigneur Band. What made that an event of some importance was that for the first time a top band was being led by a musician, a band boy, dyed in the wool and bred in the bone; somebody

37

Above, Lew Stone and Jack Jackson; right, Lew Stone and band transport. The elephant was recruited to augment the trumpets

who cared more for the music the band was making than for the shape of his white tie or the width of his trouser bottoms. Lew Stone was well into his thirties when the coveted baton passed into his hands. But he was vastly experienced, and what is more important, he possessed a rare talent – he was an arranger of taste and invention. And the arrangements, the orchestration of popular tunes, tailored to suit a particular combination of players, were, by 1932, really becoming the name of the game.

To the combination of three saxes, three brass and four rhythm that he had inherited from Roy Fox, Lew Stone added a second trombone to make four brass, and a second tenor to make four saxes. The function of these augmentations was not to make the band louder, but to deepen and enrich the orchestral texture, taking advantage of the lessons to be learned from the recordings, now flowing in a steady stream from America, by such bands as Fletcher Henderson, Duke Ellington, Don Redman, Count Basie and the Casa Loma Orchestra.

It is worth noting the personnel of the 1932–33 Lew Stone band. Alfie Noakes and Nat Gonella were on trumpets, Joe Ferrie and Lew Davis, trombones. Joe Crossman and Ernest Ritte, alto saxophones, Harry Berly and Jim Easton, tenors. The rhythm section was Lew Stone leading from the piano, Tiny Winters on bass, Bill Harty on drums, and Al Bowlly, the guitarist, as vocalist. Al Bowlly was swiftly to become the nation's favourite crooner. Nat Gonella, whose looks were equal parts choirboy and

Above, Roy Fox at the
Monseigneur (Lew Stone is
the pianist, Al Bowlly the
guitarist); right, Nat Gonella,
doubtless with Georgia on
his mind; and, far right,
Ambrose in the film 'Soft
Lights and Sweet Music',
with the Dorchester Girls

street fighter, was so besotted by the playing and singing of Louis Armstrong that he parlayed his adulation into an entire career. His love for that great musician was genuine and deeply felt, and his own gifts, his instinct for jazz and his playing technique were by no means negligible; and while the *cognoscenti* might scoff, declaring his efforts (not without wit) a pale imitation of the immortal Satchelmouth, the public at large took his 'Georgia' and his 'Minnie The Moocher' to their hearts.

Tiny Winters, the bass player, had the build of a jockey and the voice of a man shouting at you from the top of a mountain. His contributions to the Lew Stone repertoire in such numbers as 'Little Nell' and 'Annie Doesn't Live Here Anymore' added greatly to the resounding success of those late-night broadcasts.

In 1934, when Al Bowlly and Bill Harty left to join Ray Noble in New York, their places on the bandstand were filled by Albert Harris on guitar and Jock Jacobsen on drums. And Lew Stone relinquished the piano to Stanley Black. The loss of Al Bowlly as the band's singer was a blow, but it must be said that these changes vastly improved that section of a dance band which is its rhythmic heartbeat.

Ambrose. Of all the jobs available to dance band musicians, the one most coveted was to be in Ambrose's orchestra. It wasn't that he paid the best money, which he did; the fact was, he demanded the very best and got it. To be a member of the Ambrose orchestra was to have made it to the top, to attract the envy and the admiration of one's fellow professionals. Quite simply, Ambrose and his Orchestra was the best that London had to offer.

Bert Ambrose himself would never have claimed to be the world's greatest musician; over the years the fiddle playing had grown more and more perfunctory, and it is doubtful if a page of orchestral score meant any more to him than a page of Sanskrit. But he knew what was good when he heard it and would settle for nothing less. And if the boys didn't love him, and that would have been asking too much, at the very least there was a mutual respect.

He, too, had talented arrangers in the band. Sid Phillips, who played neat, expert and razzle-dazzle clarinet, also provided the intricate and musicianly scores which featured prominently in those famous Saturday night broadcasts. And Bert Barnes, the band's pianist, he of the petulant lip and the basilisk eye, wrote arrangements that were both elegant and gutsy. Others in the band were Max Goldberg, quite the best lead trumpet player in the business, strong as a lion and solid as a rock; Danny Pola, an American who played exciting, Chicago-style clarinet; and Max Bacon, the band's drummer, who, before he turned full-time comic, was just right for the band and for the times. It was only later, with the advent of the Swing Bands, that Max's drumming was made to sound corny.

Henry Hall. Odd man out among all the regularly broadcasting bands of the 'thirties was the official BBC Dance Orchestra itself, whose leader was Henry Hall. Because of their resident status they got more air time than any of the bands, and yet, had you asked a musician of the time for his opinion of their music, you would have received a very rude answer indeed. For it was the judgement of their peers that what the BBC Dance Orchestra played was a good deal more BBC than Dance Orchestra; that it was, even at its best, insipid, spineless schmaltz. Such opinions among musicians, grimly held and vociferously expressed, did not prevent Henry Hall from becoming one of the nation's prime favourites. And for those same musicians there could be no more conclusive proof of the rising power of broadcasting as the decade advanced.

That such views were coloured by just the merest tint of jealousy, there can be no doubt. But big time West End musicians always were a pretty uncharitable bunch where their professional status was concerned. They resented strangers, could spot them with unerring instinct – and Henry Hall's was a band of strangers. He had first formed it in Scotland, at Gleneagles, the famous golfing hotel. It had been one of the very first bands to do an outside broadcast, way back in 1924. Hall was later oppointed Musical Director of all the London Midland and Scottish railway hotels, of which Gleneagles was, mixing the metaphor, the flagship. When in 1932, to the astonishment and chagrin of his London rivals, he landed the plum job of leading a BBC Dance Orchestra (Jack Payne, who had held the job since 1928, was leaving to take his band on tour), it was his little six-piece combination that he brought down with him, augmented for the occasion, but still bearing the unmistakable stamp of its origins beside the nineteenth hole at Gleneagles. All agreed that Henry Hall was a thoroughly nice man. He looked and sounded like a

RADIO TIMES

Photograph by
Cannons of
Hollywood

A New Dance Tune
Written and Composed
by
HENRY HALL

Within the last few days listeners
have heard the B.B.C. Dance
Orchestra play Henry Hall's new
number, 'Radio Times'. It is appropriate for us to present our
readers, this Christmas, with a
facsimile copy of Henry Hall's
original manuscript of the tune,
which will be found on the following
two pages written clearly enough
for you to play it on your piano.

**Henry Hall, broadcasting in
1933. In those days you got
dressed up just to be heard**

Fred Elizalde and his great Savoy Band. Elizalde is at the piano, and from left to right the musicians are: Dick Maxwell, banjo; Len Fillis, guitar; Adrian Rollini, bass sax; Ronnie Gubertini, drums; Reg Owen, tenor sax; Norman Payne, trumpet; Chelsea Quealey, trumpet; Harry Hayes and Bobby Davis, alto saxes

prep school housemaster, and when it was discovered that he had gained his earliest musical experience with the Salvation Army, everyone said that it explained much about the way the band sounded. They giggled and shrugged, cursed the fogies and fuddy-duddies who ran the Corporation, and prayed for a change of reign in those remote corridors of power. Alas, it didn't come until after the war, in time for Radio One and the Pop Revolution; too late to save the dance bands from extinction.

But to return to those earliest days of broadcasting, back in the 'twenties. There is no question at all about which band did most to form the mould into which henceforth all British dance music would be poured. It was the band of Fred Elizalde at the Savoy Hotel.

Elizalde was a well-born Spaniard, born in Manila and brought up in the United States, who came to Cambridge as an undergraduate and was soon involved in the nascent jazz enthusiasms which were already shaking those hallowed halls. In 1927, he and his band were broadcasting from the Savoy, and for the first time the British were listening to music that sounded suspiciously like the real thing. He had raided American bands for his key musicians; wild, hard-drinking men, carriers of the torch and bearers of the message. Even their names were strange and romantic sounding; Fud Livingston, Chelsea Quealey, Adrian Rollini. Livingston played clarinet, Quealey, the trumpet, and Rollini, the most elaborate piece of plumbing ever devised for musical expression, the bass sax. Like all cultural invasions, this one did much to incite the natives to emulation. In the band were two young Englishmen who were to be among the best jazz players the country would produce – Norman Payne on trumpet, and Harry Hayes on alto sax.

What, in short, the Elizalde band did was play jazz. The British however, always hesitant to cross those wild frontiers, were somewhat less than enchanted. The paying customers at the Savoy complained that the band was difficult to dance to; radio audiences complained that they couldn't recognise their favourite tunes, dressed up as they were in the filigreed finery of a jazz orchestration. By the spring of 1929, Elizalde was off the air, and by July he was out of the Savoy.

Only one group gave this marvellous band their unstinted admiration and approval, the small but rapidly growing coterie of dance band *aficionados*, whose bible was the weekly musical magazine, the *Melody Maker*. When, in November 1928, the 'M.M' ran its annual Best Band Poll, they voted Elizalde their number one. They at least had been glued to their radios for his broadcasts and had sensed that something new and exciting was happening in the world of music.

It is not going too far to suggest that had there been somebody (anybody!) at the BBC with taste and discernment enough to distinguish a good dance band from a bad one, we might have suffered less of Henry Hall's smug, insular and witless contributions, and British dance music might have reached maturity a good deal sooner than it did.

In 1922, Harrods were enlisting exhibition dancers to help sell their gramophones

For the record

IN 1889, EMILE BERLINER INVENTED
a disc, ten inches in diameter, and made of black hardened wax, which
would go round on a gramophone turntable at seventy-eight revolutions a
minute, thus reproducing for a duration of roughly three minutes whatever you cared to record. In 1911, Irving Berlin knocked off a little tune
called 'Alexander's Ragtime Band', and among those who hastened to
commit to the record this palpable hit was a Continental outfit working in
England and calling themselves Gottlieb's Orchestra. This they did in the
studios of His Master's Voice, and the resulting sound resembled nothing
so much as the seven dwarfs descending the Cresta Run while playing the
kazoo and beating their overcoats with rolled up newspapers.

However, that doesn't seem to have unduly upset the paying customers, who bought the record, wound up gramophones with cornucopia-like
horns, changed their steel needles and jigged and shimmied to the tinny
music, right through the war years and into the roaring 'twenties.

Poor Herr Gottlieb, doubtless *persona non grata* from 1914 to 1918, was
replaced by others; Olley Oakley, wizard of the banjo, and his Syncopated
Five, who recorded such numbers as 'The Vamp', and 'By The Camp
Fire', on the Edison Bell Winner label; and the Corner House Ragtime
Band, stars of Joe Lyons' lavish and popular new tea rooms, with such

Recording stars of the 'twenties: Al Starita (top left), Debroy Somers (bottom left), and Jack Hylton (right)

items as 'Goodbye Dixie', and 'They're Wearing 'Em Higher In Hawaii'.

By 1921 the first of the recording giants had arrived on the scene. He was a Lancashire lad named Jack Hylton, who, after an apprenticeship served in seaside concert party, touring pantomime, at the cinema organ and in army entertainments, found himself in London leading a band on the roof of the Queen's Hall in Langham Place, and recording for HMV at their studios at Hayes in Middlesex. And not only that. Within a year he was also recording, as Jack Hylton's Jazz Band and the Embassy Dance Orchestra on the Zonophone label, and as the Ariel Dance Orchestra on Ariel. He was thirty years of age and the best was yet to come.

But Jack Hylton was not to have the new record-buying market all to himself. With the beginning of broadcasting in 1923, the Savoy bands – the Havana, the Orpheans and Fred Elizalde – were there to provide competition. So were Ambrose and his Embassy Club Orchestra. The Savoy Orpheans, led by Debroy Somers, and including in its ranks such bright American stars as Al and Ray Starita and Carroll Gibbons, were offering gems like 'Horsey, Keep Your Tail Up', 'When It's Night Time In Italy It's Wednesday Over Here', 'Say It With A Ukulele', and 'I Love You (Little Jesse James)'. Ambrose contributed 'China Boy Go Sleep', 'Innocent Lonesome Blue Baby', and 'The Birth Of The Blues' with a vocal chorus by the Hamilton Sisters and Fordyce.

In 1925, there came a real technological breakthrough – electrical recording. Sound quality improved dramatically; the great horned speakers disappeared, gramophones became neat and portable and as ubiquitous as today's transistor radios. The music was going round and round and coming out just about everywhere. Jack Hylton made the first electrical recordings for HMV in June of that year. Among the titles were, 'Yes Sir, That's My Baby', 'I'll See You In My Dreams', and 'Paddlin' Madelin' Home'.

That same year, a violinist named Alfredo, who had recently left Jack Hylton to try his luck with his own band, started to record for Edison Bell Winner, such titles as 'Fascinating Rhythm' and 'Lady Be Good', and his records were to remain popular until 1930. The Savoy Havana Band on Columbia offered 'When My Sugar Walks Down The Street' with a vocal chorus by Cyril Ramon Newton, and Herman Darewski, Percival Mackey and Jack Payne all made their recording débuts.

Of these last, Jack Payne's was the band that would make the strongest and the most lasting impression. He was broadcasting regularly from the Hotel Cecil in 1925, and when in 1928 he was appointed Director of Dance Music for the BBC, his future was assured. In 1927 he was busily recording on the Regal label and contributing to the general merriment such items as 'Ain't She Sweet?', 'It Made You Happy When You Made Me Cry', and 'Since Tommy Atkins Taught The Chinese How To Charleston'. That same year also saw the beginnings of a career for young Harry Roy, featured with his brother Syd's Lyricals; while Jack Hylton offered the record-buying public his version of 'Me And Jane In A Plane', 'Ain't That A Grand And Glorious Feeling', and 'Flat Tyred Papa, Mamma's Gonna Give You Air'.

In 1928 the names of Charlie Kunz and Billy Cotton could be added to your record shopping list, and in 1930 the crooners were beginning to make themselves heard; Al Bowlly, first with Fred Elizalde and now with Percival Mackey's Band, Sam Browne with Ray Starita, Les Allan with Pete Mandell, Val Rosing with Billy Cotton, and Ella Logan (later to enchant Broadway with 'How Are Things In Gloccamorra?') with Ambrose.

By 1930 the trickle of recordings from the United States had become a steady flow, and whatever the public at large might have thought of this music, the musicians themselves were being profoundly influenced by what they heard. On the one hand there were the sickly sweet *vibrato*-wracked saxophones of Guy Lombardo, the opulent over-orchestrated pomposities of Paul Whiteman, and the slickly efficient 'commercial jazz' arrangements of the Casa Loma Orchestra; nothing startlingly new there, just a few cute musical tricks, but the bands of Maurice Winnick, Jack Hylton and Ambrose were quick to add them to their respective repertoires. On the other hand . . . well now, that was something else. In that first year of the new decade, Parlophone began to issue a series of records which they dubbed 'The New Rhythm Style Series', and the first coupling

Tell the Advertiser you saw it in " RECORDS."

Jack Payne and the BBC Dance Orchestra in 1928

A rare photograph of Louis Armstrong and his Hot Five in 1926

available was 'West End Blues' played by Louis Armstrong and his Hot Five, and 'Freeze And Melt' by Eddie Lang's Orchestra. When banjoists heard the guitar playing of Eddie Lang, they hung their instruments on the wall, or threw them into a corner to join the sousaphone already there and as extinct as the Great Auk. And after they had heard the opening cadenza of 'West End Blues', well, trumpet playing was never to be the same again.

There followed recordings of the great black bands: Fletcher Henderson, Don Redman, Count Basie and Duke Ellington. And the dazzling invention of such instrumentalists as Benny Goodman, the Dorsey brothers, Jack Teagarden and Bix Beiderbecke. And Frankie Trumbauer and Joe Venuti, and the whole galaxy of the new jazz virtuosi. British musicians realised that here was a whole new language, one that would have to be studied, practised, learned and reproduced. Although it might be years before much of it could be put to use in the nightly grind at hotel, Palais or nightclub, the message was clear – the masters of their craft were elsewhere, in New York, Chicago and Los Angeles, and henceforth the British dance bands would have to hurry and narrow the gap whose physical form was the Atlantic Ocean, but whose cultural distance could be measured only in light years, or for ever remain stuck in the mud of that musical backwater which was the rest of Europe.

In 1931 and 1932, titles by the newly famous radio dance bands began to appear in the record shops. Roy Fox, Harry Roy, Lew Stone and

Ambrose all repeated in the recording studios the successes they were having on the air, and soon recognised a simple equation: the more times you broadcast a number, the more records of it you were likely to sell. The age of the song plugger had arrived.

Roy Fox recorded his signature tune, 'Whispering', featuring his pretty muted trumpet, then launched Al Bowlly upon his glittering career with such songs as 'Sweet And Lovely', 'Just One More Chance' and 'You're My Everything'. And Nat Gonella planted himself firmly in the national consciousness playing and singing such numbers as 'Oh Monah', 'Georgia On My Mind' and 'I'll Be Glad When You're Dead You Rascal You'. Harry Roy got started on the road to fame with his strident vocalising of 'Nobody's Sweetheart Now' and 'Somebody Stole My Gal'. Lew Stone, investing his recent inheritance of Roy Fox's Monseigneur Band, doubled his money with novelty numbers like 'Little Nell' and 'Who's Afraid Of The Big Bad Wolf?' in which Tiny Winters, Nat Gonella, Joe Ferrie and Jim Easton all joined in the simple fun. Al Bowlly enhanced his reputation with 'Close Your Eyes' and 'Brother, Can You Spare A Dime?', and Stanley Black's brilliant arrangements of 'Blue Jazz' and 'White Jazz' put the band through their instrumental paces.

Ambrose presented his vocalists, Sam Browne and Elsie Carlisle, the former in 'Peanut Vendor' and 'You Forgot Your Gloves', the latter in 'Pu-leeze, Mister Hemingway' and 'Little Man You've Had A Busy Day', and put them together in potent partnership for 'Let's Put Out The Lights And Go To Sleep' and 'No No, A Thousand Times No (I'd Rather Die Than Say Yes)'.

The song was Ambrose's signature tune. Below right, Harry Roy and his Mayfair Hotel Band, with his featured singers, Bill Currie and Ivor Moreton

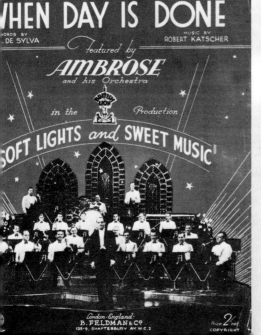

A goodly piece of the recording action was being carved off by the peripatetic Jack Hylton. In 1931 he scored a palpable hit with a thing called 'Rhymes', a collection of faintly scatological limericks, each followed by the lusty refrain: 'That was a beautiful rhyme, sing us another one, do'. Which of course the singer (J.H. himself) obligingly did. 'Rhymes' was probably the first popular song to occupy both sides of a record, as parts one and two, and so successful was it that the following year Hylton recorded its sequel, called unsurprisingly, 'More Rhymes'. Leslie Sarony, the author of this protean work, who was busily writing comedy songs for just about everybody, followed up 'Rhymes' with another hit for Hylton called 'He Played The Ukulele As The Ship Went Down'.

For dance band musicians, recording was the icing on the cake. A steady job in the West End paid well; salaries ranged between fifteen and twenty-five pounds a week in the mid-'thirties. But a session in a recording studio was worth three pounds, and a couple of those a week made all the difference to the take-home pay. A recording session lasted for three hours, and the aim was to record four titles within that time. It wasn't easy. In those 78 rpm days, before the introduction of magnetic tape, recordings were inscribed on wax masters. None of today's wizardry was available then: you got it right all the way through, or you did it all over again. Many were the frustrating, nerve-jangling moments when, having successfully negotiated two minutes and fifty-five seconds of the number's ultimate three-minute duration, a trumpet player would hit a clinker, or a

Jack Hylton and his Band in 1933. Dave Shand and Freddie Schweitzer are the middle two in the saxophone section (see chapter 6)

clarinettist emit a fearful ear-piercing reed squeak. The band would stop playing and glare at the culprit, muttering the while a few choice musicianly epithets, before embarking on take three or four, five or six.

Most name-band musicians could rely upon the occasional session in the recording studios to augment their incomes, but the real élite of the business, the aristocrats of the dance band world, were the session boys, that small exclusive group of virtuosi who recorded not only with their regular bands but, on such mornings and afternoons as were left to them, with other bands as well. They did the film sessions too; providing background music for the movies was nice work if you could get it, and those who did could boost their incomes way up into the fifty-pound-a-week bracket.

The skills demanded of such musicians were prodigious; impeccable sight reading, flawless technique, iron discipline. In terms of pure instrumental ability, they were the best. And they were the men called upon by those bandleaders who made their entire careers in the production of records. Jay Wilbur was such a bandleader. He was staff director for the Dominion label, and later for the Crystalate Company which produced Imperial and Rex records. But the king of them all was Ray Noble.

Noble was musical director for HMV records from 1929 to 1934. He was a talented arranger and a composer of some distinction. Two of his songs 'Love Is The Sweetest Thing', and 'Goodnight Sweetheart', were among the very few written by an Englishman to challenge the virtual monopoly by Americans in popular songwriting. His recordings with

SEE THAT

YOU GET THE SOUNDBOX THAT PLAYS FACE

DOWNWARDS

The 8TH Wonder

Make it a 'WONDER' Summe

Not only in sweetness and volume of tone but in portability and value is the marked superiority of this amazing Portable revealed. Comparison will show that the "Wonder" Portable Model of the Cliftophone is not only far ahead of other portables but of many cabinet models.

Specification:—Complete Internal Horn. PLAYS WITH LID CLOSED. Holds nine 12" records. Size 12½" × 12½" × 7½". Weight 14 lb. Finish'd in Black Leatherette. Garrard Motor new type, extra strong single spring. 10" turntable, plays 12" records. Nickelled fittings. Cliftophone Sound Box with new type Tone Arm. Price 5 gns.

The "WONDER" PORTABLE MODEL of

The Cliftophone

Brings any Gramophone Up-to-date

The "Cliftophone" Telescopic Tone Arm with Sound Box will fit most gramophones, and will in practically every instance make the instrument far better than ever **3 gns.** before.

Any Music Store will be pleased to Demonstrate. In case of difficulty write to us for the name and address of nearest dealer.

CHAPPELL PIANO CO. LTD.,
50 NEW BOND ST., LONDON, W.1

WIDER RANGE - FINER TONE - MORE PERFECT PORTABILITY

Tell the Advertiser you saw it in " RECORDS."

Portable gramophones in 1927. Note the price – five guineas. If you don't know what guineas are, you are too young to have owned one. Above, a very early Ray Noble Band.

what was called The New Mayfair Orchestra were so successful that HMV were persuaded to disregard a cherished tradition and name the leader of what was essentially a 'house band', and release his records as played by Ray Noble and his Orchestra.

A listing of the musicians who played for Ray Noble during his years at HMV reads like a roll call of champions. Among them were Max Goldberg, Norman Payne, Alfie Noakes, Nat Gonella, trumpets; Tony Thorpe and Lew Davis, trombones; Freddie Gardner, Laurie Payne, Bob Wise, Reg Pink, saxophones; Albert Harris, Dave Thomas, guitar; Tiny Winters, bass; Harry Jacobson, piano; Bill Harty, drums; Reg Pursglove and Eric Siday, violins. And of course, Al Bowlly, his star vocalist.

The sale of gramophone records in the 'twenties and 'thirties never achieved the dazzling multiples that have become almost commonplace in the post-war years, when golden discs, signifying the sale of a million copies, adorn the living quarters of such as Elvis Presley and the Beatles like soup plates in an Italian kitchen. What those ten-inch black discs happily have done is leave us an indelible record of the dance music of those times, as bright and as fresh as the morning when the light in the studio glowed 'steady red' and the boys blew the notes.

The wee small hours

IN 1924, AROUND TWO O'CLOCK IN the morning, when the last waltz had been played at London's hotels and restaurants, those diners and dancers who had not yet had their fill of merrymaking would take themselves off to one or another of the nightclubs that since the end of the war had sprung up all over the West End. It is impossible to say just how many of these places existed at any given time, since they opened and closed with such alarming frequency that would-be celebrants, arriving at their favourite haunt, might find themselves facing nothing but a grimly padlocked front door, and be greeted by a furtive individual handing out grubby cards announcing that London's newest and most exciting *boîte de nuit* had opened for business that very night in a cosy basement just around the corner.

It will, however, serve as a useful guide to know that between the years 1924 and 1928, sixty-five such clubs were prosecuted for selling drinks after hours. For the plain fact was that all this nocturnal activity was, quite simply, illegal. The licensing laws of the time provided for the sale of intoxicating liquor after the hour of 11.00 p.m. only if food was served at the same time, and such licence was never granted to extend beyond 2.00 a.m. Anybody providing or consuming the hard stuff after that hour was doing so on unlicensed premises and thus breaking the law. And since the *raison d'être* of a nightclub was to supply incorrigible revellers, chronic insomniacs and dedicated stop-outs with liquid refreshment until such time as they either fell down or ran out of money, all the clubs operated in that limbo land which led straight to Savile Row Police Station.

It went like this: from time to time the police, having lined up their targets for the night, would descend upon them in some strength, and having gained entry, as they say in their reports, would proceed to arrest everybody in sight. One moment the band would be playing, the bubbly would be flowing, the fun would be fast and furious – the next, all present would be headed via the Black Maria for an uncomfortable night in the cells. It should be said that none of those involved regarded these shenanigans with too much seriousness, least of all the miscreant proprietors, who, having paid their fines and seen their premises firmly padlocked, might spend an hour or two looking for yet another noisome cellar, large enough to accommodate a few chairs and tables, an upright piano and a kit of drums, and would very often be open for business at 'London's newest and most exciting' that very same night.

Undisputed queen of all this nocturnal activity during the 'twenties was an extraordinary woman named Kate Meyrick. Mrs Meyrick, 'Ma' to her loyal patrons, was the daughter of an Irish doctor, whose errant husband had left her with a house in Brighton, six children and no visible means of supporting them. She opened her first nightclub, the Cecil, later to become notorious as the Forty-Three Club (for its address in Gerrard Street), and was soon the proprietress of three or four thriving establishments. It is a measure of her success that between 1924 and 1928, when Sir William Joynson-Hicks, the Home Secretary of the day, was closing nightclubs with such determined enthusiasm, Mrs Meyrick's Forty-Three Club was not raided once. The reason for such miraculous immunity was revealed, alas, when the Sergeant Goddard case broke. The unfortunate sergeant was found to have saved an embarrassingly large amount of money out of his modest pay as a zealous and conscientious member of the vice squad. Mrs Meyrick went to prison for fifteen months. She was to return to the West End, but was never again quite to recapture those days of glory.

The bands that played at those clubs, Mrs Meyrick's and others', were small, seldom more than five pieces, and consisting usually of piano, drums and bass (sousaphone in those earlier days), saxophone and trumpet. They were a reckless bunch, those nightclub musicians; hard drinking, loose living, and as predatory as any of that night-blooming species – waiters, dance hostesses, doormen and chuckers-out – who made their living fleecing the toffs whose pleasure it was not to go to bed before dawn. One saxophone player perfected a ploy to augment his income, and it went something like this: he would contrive to be jostled by some drunken dancer reeling unsteadily on his pins past the bandstand. He would then snap the reed on his mouthpiece, emit a howl of dismay, and complain

**Kate Meyrick, the Nightclub Queen, is welcomed home from Holloway in
1930. The gentleman wearing glasses is Bob Probst, her bandleader**

that his assailant had completely destroyed his instrument. Insisting that it had been rendered totally unplayable, he would demand payment for a new one. The befuddled and now contrite gentleman would cough up twenty pounds or so and beg forgiveness. That a saxophone reed (a sliver of shaped cane), while being indispensable for producing sound from that instrument, was at the same time replaceable at the cost of something like sixpence, would be a fact known only to the rest of the band, who were, need it be said, not about to reveal the secret. How often this particular gambit could be employed by the same saxophonist, and in the same club, is not recorded.

The nightclub musicians started work at 11.00 at night, played until 4.00, sometimes 5.00 a.m., then slept until mid-afternoon. They could go for weeks in wintertime without ever seeing the light of day. As the 'twenties proceeded and the popularity of dance music spread to the hotels and restaurants, the ballrooms and music halls; as the ranks of the musicians swelled to answer the new demand; and as their skills increased and were refined to meet the requirements of a music beginning to come of age, so the nightclub musicians became a more clearly recognisable group. They were, on the one hand, those whose abilities did not extend to the reading of band parts, which were fast becoming more difficult and complex; and on the other, the dedicated jazz musicians whose devotion to what they regarded as a new art form would not permit them to sit nightly on some restaurant bandstand and play oom ching for an audience, middle-aged and middle-class, who could not appreciate and would not tolerate their kind of music.

The early 'thirties were a bad time for the night spots. Relentless harrassment by the police, following the acute embarrassment of Sergeant Goddard, was making life impossible for the club owners. The British licensing laws and their dogged enforcement were spoiling everybody's fun, and Paris, with champagne at reasonable prices, the Folies Bergères, not to mention legalised brothels, was a mere hour and a half away by Imperial Airways. Then, in 1936, some unsung genius invented the bottle party, a device which for simplicity and effectiveness must surely rank alongside the lightning zip fastener and the sliced loaf.

The bottle party dodge worked in the following way: since drinking and dancing on unlicensed public premises was forbidden, the room in which the nightly festivities took place was assumed to be private, and the customers to be guests of the owner. These 'guests', all 'friends' of the chap who owned the place, would be asked upon arrival to pay, not an entrance fee or cover charge, but simply a little something towards the night's expenses, after which they were welcome to enter and enjoy such amenities as their compulsively gregarious 'host' had provided. However, if this occasion should happen to be the first time the 'guest' had been 'invited' to this particular 'party', he would, a million regrets, not be able to buy a drink, since the 'host', not being a man of trade, but, you understand, simply a chap with an insatiable urge to entertain his friends,

Cabaret time at the Kit Cat

did not sell drink. However, there *was* a friendly neighbourhood wine merchant who *did* sell drink, and he would be happy, upon receipt of an order to do so, to deliver to this very spot, at any hour of day or night, as many bottles as the 'guest' felt that he could handle. Of course the order would take a little time to fill, say, twenty-four hours, after which the 'guest' could show up on any night of his choice, demand one bottle of something from the great number of bottles he had previously ordered (the usual order was one dozen of Scotch, one dozen of gin, and one dozen of brandy), and drink himself insensible if that was what amused him. To complete the charade, when upon arrival the 'guest' would ask for the bottle of his choice, a man would take his order and convey it, usually by bicycle, to the premises of the friendly neighbourhood wine merchant (who had stayed open all night for this very purpose), where the stock of liquor previously ordered by the 'guest' was most conveniently stored. The man would grab the appropriate bottle, mount his bicycle and

Adelaide Hall (who once sang with Duke Ellington) entertains the customers at the Florida Club in Mayfair

hot-pedal it back to the club – oops, sorry, the private party, where the 'guest' was waiting, presumably with his tongue hanging out. Provided mine 'host' did not become either lazy or greedy, and sell a drink to one of the minions of the law, who, instantly recognisable though they invariably were, were for ever haunting the joint in the hope of catching him out, his 'private party' and the premises in which he chose to give it were safe from prosecution.

Pioneer of the bottle parties was the Florida Club, just off Berkeley Square, a cosy *boîte* with a multi-coloured glass dance floor, where Gerry Moore, who looked remarkably like the Emperor Haile Selassie of Ethiopia, led the band from his piano. And in no time at all a whole new generation of nightclubs, emboldened by their new freedom from the attentions of the law, were opening up all over town. At the up-market end of the spectrum there were lavishly appointed rooms with sizeable bands and elaborate floor shows, like The Cocoanut Grove and The Paradise, both of them in Regent Street. In these and in others, like the ultra-

Alice Delysia, a star of musical comedy, entertains her friends at the Kit Cat. That's Sophie Tucker enjoying it in the background

exclusive '400' club, the music provided was simply more of what the revellers had danced to earlier in the evening in the hotels and at the smart restaurants. The bands might be somewhat smaller, usually eight or nine pieces (relieved from time to time by a frilly-shirted rhumba band), but the style of playing and the music played, that endless conveyor belt of Cole Porter, Gershwin and Richard Rodgers tunes, was the same. The well-heeled clientele simply moved on from one place to the other and hardly noticed the difference.

It was at the other end of the spectrum that the true nightclub spirit asserted itself. In the basements below dress shops and Italian cafés, in the streets and alleys around Piccadilly and Soho, in the clip joints with their scruffy waiters, peroxided hostesses and I-have-an-uncle-in-the-Mafia proprietors, that's where the real musical action was. Most of these places employed the statutory five-piece band, a group that would be augmented and enhanced as night-time shaded into the wee small hours by musicians who, their nights' work over in the West End restaur-

ants, drifted thither, attracted as to some musical oasis, there to refresh their spirits and flex their instrumental muscles; in short, to 'sit in' and play a little jazz.

Nobody really knows just when the jam session, as it came to be known, first made its appearance in the West End of London. By the mid-'twenties it already was an honoured institution in the bordellos of New Orleans and the speakeasies of New York and Chicago. It is safe to assume that by the end of the decade the habit had crossed the Atlantic and was firmly established among our indigenous jazzmen. Certainly by the time the bottle parties had opened their doors for business, the proprietors of such places had accepted it as normal practice, providing a table for the visiting (and unpaid) musicians and even, in the case of the more benign of that predatory ilk, an occasional drink.

Clubs during the 'thirties where a jam session was usually under way by 3.00 a.m. were The Manhattan, The Bag O'Nails, The Bat Club, The Nut House, The Blue Lagoon, The Shim Sham and The Nest. Of these, by far the most interesting and exciting was The Nest. Housed in a basement in

A rare moment of repose at the Nest Club. Duncan Whyte, the guru of righteous jazz, is at the microphone; the trombonist with the faraway look is George Chisholm; and the Billy Bunter on the right is Derek Neville, a manic baritone sax player

Kingly Street, behind the stately façades of Regent Street, it was exclusively the preserve of London's then tiny black community; a microcosmic Harlem in the heart of town. Such whites as ventured down its precipitate staircase to sniff the marijuana-scented air, gawp at the uninhibited high spirits of the habitués, and enjoy for breakfast the best corned beef hash in Europe, were the usual thrill-seeking West Enders, perhaps a sociologist or two, but above all, the jazz musicians. For it was Nestwards that visiting black musicians, here to tour the music halls, or to fulfil such other engagements that were open to them, always gravitated at the end of their day's work. There one might find, at one time or another, Louis Armstrong, Art Tatum, Coleman Hawkins, members of the Duke Ellington band like Johnny Hodges, Sonny Greer and Barney Bigard, Garland Wilson and Fats Waller.

On a night when such as these were in town, the word would circulate: 'So and so will be at the Nest tonight. Be there!' And on such memorable occasions the room would burst at the seams, and the music would throb beneath the pavement of Kingly Street until long after dawn.

DANCING

TAUGHT BY EXPERTS OF CHAMPIONSHIP RANK

Individual tuition in every Ballroom dance, including "The Rhythm Step," "The Yale Blues," "Black Bottom," the new "Quick Time" and the important modification in the "New Waltz."

Staff :

GIPSEY STRUDWICK
(Principal)

Nancy Bramall Frank Ford
Dorothy Cole Joan Corfield
Audrey Staples W. Tacey
H. Barrington Evans

Fees : 10/6 each lesson.
or £2 : 12 : 6 for six.

'Phone :
PARK
5220

APPLY : DANCE SECRETARY

EMPRESS ROOMS

ROYAL PALACE HOTEL, KENSINGTON, LONDON, W.

'Do you come here often?'

TO GO FROM THE SAVOY HOTEL TO the Hammersmith Palais is to go from caviar to cod's roe, from white tie and tails to blue serge and winkle pickers, from *haute coiffure* to home perms. For the Palais is where the man in the street has been going for over half a century to enjoy the energetic relaxation of ballroom dancing, and it was at their local Palais that most people first heard the new post-war popular music played by a modern dance band.

The Hammersmith Palais de Danse opened its doors in 1919 and the crowds flocked in to sample its many splendours; a sprung maple floor, forty dance instructresses, uniformed attendants, ladies' and gents' toilets of unheard-of opulence, a mirrored sphere which revolved under filtered spotlights to turn the vast hall into a dappled, multi-coloured wonderland. There was a huge bandstand, raised high above the throng, and framed in a half-shell of fluted plaster, which made the dinner-jacketed musicians look like a tableau staged by Sandro Botticelli himself.

Among the first attractions to occupy this splendid setting was a group of musicians fresh from triumphs in their American homeland. They called themselves The Original Dixieland Jazz Band, although they were not from Dixieland, did not play jazz, and were not remarkably original. They were, in fact, five young men who played piano, drums, clarinet,

69

trumpet and trombone, wore white top hats and dazzled and delighted the dancers of Hammersmith with their rags and foxtrots, and with newfangled dances called The Charleston, The Shimmy and The Grizzly Bear.

The dancers shuffled and hopped, leapt and pranced, suffered bruised ankles and grazed knees in a desperate effort to keep abreast of the strange and outlandish rhythms they were being called upon to master. And a new professional, equal to the occasion, began to emerge. He was the teacher/demonstrator of the brand new art of modern ballroom dancing. In the West End, the tea dancers at the Savoy, the Café de Paris and the

OH! MOTHER I'M WILD!

By
HOWARD JOHNSON,
HARRY PEASE AND EDDIE NELSON.

Featured by the ·

Photo by Hana Studios, Ltd

ORIGINAL DIXIELAND JAZZ BAND.

Copyright.   Price 2/- net

HERMAN DAREWSKI MUSIC PUBLISHING Co
ST SWITHIN'S SYNDICATE, LTD.
INCORPORATING CHARLES SHEARD & Co
122, 124 & 142, CHARING CROSS ROAD, LONDON, W.C.2.
AMERICA — LEO FEIST, INC. NEW YORK.

PRINTED IN ENGLAND

Piccadilly Hotel were avidly watching a gentleman who called himself Santos Casani, and who looked like a bantam Erich Von Stroheim, complete with monocle and haughty demeanour. Once, with his partner, he demonstrated the Charleston standing atop a London taxicab cruising Kingsway, an event which, captured on newsreel film, was to become an essential prop for nostalgic television programmes.

The Dance Palaces had Victor Sylvester. His father was a vicar in Wembley and he had learned to dance because the Bishop of London held an annual ball at Lambeth Palace for the sons of the clergy. He was tall, muscular and athletic, and had the bland anonymous good looks of an

The famous snap of Santos Casani and his partner Charlestoning along Kingsway atop a London taxi. Note: the 177 bus no longer goes to Kings Cross. Right, Mr and Mrs Victor Sylvester

officer of the Blues. So completely did he master the intricacies of the new dance steps that in 1922 he became World Professional Ballroom Champion, the most famous dancer in Britain and the envy of every Palais-goer who had ever sidled along that seemingly endless row of bentwood chairs whereon sat the unattended ladies, and mumbled, 'Excuse me, but may I have the next waltz?'

By 1924, a body calling itself the Imperial Society of Dance Teachers, having sat in solemn conclave and decided that dancers in ballrooms were unruly, ill-disciplined (having too good a time?), and in need of expert instruction, decreed that henceforth ballroom dancing should confine itself to four basic steps: the waltz, the foxtrot, the quick-step and the tango. Sylvester, as befits a son of the manse, perceived the virtue of this edict, and in 1928 he charted, codified and enshrined the new dogma in a book called *Modern Ballroom Dancing*, which since its publication has run into some fifty-five editions.

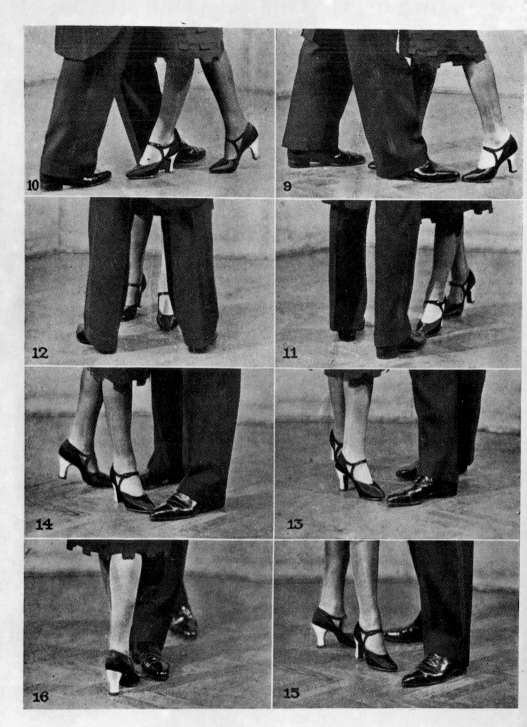

THE MODERN TANGO.

(The line of dance is from right to left).

9, 10, 11 and 12. Moving from the back " corte " to the " Promenade."
13, 14 and 15. The " Promenade " *(line of dance towards camera).* 16. From
" Promenade " back to the " Walk."

The steps are described in the text on page 820.

He opened a School of Dancing and, with his fellow pundits, added one more doctrinaire refinement. Strict tempo. Now the Palais bands were required to play music for dancing with metronomic exactitude. Any deviation, a pulse beat faster, a vibration slower, would be punished by instant banishment from the dance competitions which were proliferating around the dancing world. Dissatisfied with the musical accompaniment available, Sylvester formed his own band, dedicated to the immutability of strict tempo. Useless to complain that the music they played was insipid, rhythmically arid and harmonically bankrupt; by 1955, when rock and roll was at last beginning to blow down the walls of his impregnable Jericho, Victor Sylvester and his Orchestra had sold twenty-seven million records, more than any other British band.

By the end of the 'twenties a golden age of the Palais de Danse was beginning to dawn. London boasted The Astoria in Charing Cross Road and The Locarno in Streatham. In Manchester there was The Ritz, in Glasgow, another Locarno, in Edinburgh, The Palace. Every seaside resort had at least one dance hall; Blackpool had The Tower Ballroom, The Winter Gardens and many others. The bands that played in such places, although somewhat second-division when compared with the league leaders in the West End, were still substantial star attractions in their own world. In 1928, Billy Cotton was at The Astoria; in 1929, Jan Ralfini was at The Nottingham Palais de Danse, and Bertini was at the Tower Ballroom in Blackpool. In the early 'thirties, Billy Merrin and his Commanders were at Nottingham; Oscar Rabin and the Romany Band and Joe Loss and his Orchestra were alternating between the Astoria and Hammersmith, and vying with each other for the title of the dancers' favourite band.

If the big time musicians 'up West' had cause to complain about the lack of freedom to play the kind of music they enjoyed, the Palais bandsmen were even more grievously frustrated by the demands of a gregarious clientele bent on an evening of corporate fun and games. Competitions, demonstrations, special events, novelty numbers and latest crazes punctuated their every night's work. There were Excuse Me Foxtrots, Spot Waltzes for which prizes (compacts for the ladies, cuff links for the men) were presented to the couple who found themselves, at the end of the dance, bulls-eyed by a beam of light trained upon them from above; and there was the Paul Jones. For those too young to have participated in, or even to have witnessed that curious tribal rite, the Paul Jones was the one in which the ladies and the gentlemen (boys and girls!) formed two concentric circles which then began to move off in opposite directions to the music of 'Here We Go Gathering Nuts In May'. When the music stopped, the individual dancer coupled with whoever he or she found to be closest at hand. It is said that the marriage mart benefited hugely from such chance encounters, and it is certainly true that young men used the ballrooms as an aid to seduction, and the women as a good place to go husband hunting.

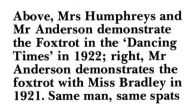

Above, Mrs Humphreys and Mr Anderson demonstrate the Foxtrot in the 'Dancing Times' in 1922; right, Mr Anderson demonstrates the foxtrot with Miss Bradley in 1921. Same man, same spats

Dancing the Paul Jones at the London Laundries Dance Championship at the Hammersmith Palais

There were nights set aside for specialised tastes: Old Tyme Nights, devoted to the preservation of the Veleta, the Polka, the Military Two-Step, and that bizarre parody of Andalusian machismo, The Paso Doble. There were Latin-American nights, consecrated to the performance of the rhumba, the conga and the Cha Cha, which in the ballroom mysteriously acquired an extra syllable and became the Char Char Char. There were the community dances that were all the rage in the middle and late 'thirties. One such was The Palais Glide, a thing of transcendental silliness which involved dancers forming a long straggling chorus line and performing kicks like half-baked Tiller Girls to the tune of 'Poor Little Angeline' ('She was just sixteen, little Angeline, always dancing on the village green . . .'). In 1937, a musical show at the Victoria Palace called *Me And My Girl* yielded a piece of bogus cockneyana by Noel Gay, called 'The Lambeth Walk'. The dance teachers took the exuberant version of cavorting pearlies and turned it into a sedate knees-up suitable for the ballroom. 'Any time you're Lambeth way, any ev'ning, any day – you'll find them all, doing the Lambeth walk. Oi!!'

They came thick and fast: 'Hands, Knees And Boomps-a-Daisy', 'Under The Spreading Chestnut Tree', 'The Hokey Cokey'. And all this simple-minded rubbish had to be supplied with musical accompaniment

77

BLUES
YALE &
BLACK BOTTOM
By Victor Silvester

Far left, dancing at the Locarno, Streatham; above, Victor Sylvester leads the band – and graphically demonstrates the Black Bottom

Kings of the Astoria,
Charing Cross Road: Joe
Loss and his Band (above)
and Oscar Rabin and the
Romany Band

by the resident band and its relentlessly smiling leader. It was no life for a grown musician. Even so, some of the Palais bands did manage to survive musically, some succeeding in becoming well-known outside the ballrooms of their nightly toil through records and broadcasting. Bertini, Jan Ralfini, Billy Merrin, Harry Leader and Lou Preager all received their modicum of air time, and their records (in strict tempo, of course) sold well to the schools of dancing and to ballroom addicts desirous of perfecting the open impetus turn and the reverse chassé in the privacy of their homes.

Most famous of all the Palais bands were Billy Cotton, Oscar Rabin and the Romany Band and Joe Loss; and since Billy Cotton's subsequent career in Variety is of greater interest, he will figure in the next chapter. The Romany Band was curiously constituted; it had virtually two bandleaders. There was Oscar Rabin himself, titular boss, seated buddha-like among the front line, honking away on his bass saxophone, and there was Harry Davis, his alter ego, handsome, elegant in tails, standing in front of the band, doing the arm waving and the smiling. The arrangement seems to have worked admirably.

Joe Loss was (and amazingly, still is) the undisputed king of the ballrooms. He was born in Liverpool in 1901, studied music in London and began his career as a violinist bandleader at The Astoria, Charing Cross Road, where his seven-piece band supplied relief for the Romany Band, who were already established stars. From 1931 until 1934 he played at The Kit Cat Club, then returned triumphantly to The Astoria to be the main attraction with a twelve-piece band. For more than thirty years Joe Loss dominated the dancing world; in 1940 it was he who led the incredible wartime boom in Palais popularity, when in the course of just one week he played to ten thousand dancers at Glasgow's Playhouse Ballroom.

The dance halls still flourish, but their numbers are sadly depleted since those hectic years, and the efforts of the bands to keep abreast of changing musical fashion have given the bandstands an oddly hybrid look; half old-fashioned Palais band, half rock and roll group. The tail-suited, bouncing, beaming bandleader, who once conducted his flock through the intricacies of the Palais Glide and the Hokey Cokey, can now be listed among the endangered species. He is all but gone from the scene.

Jack Hylton 'and his boys', as the French would have them, assembled in front of the Paris Opera in 1931. Shades of Pergolesi and Haydn look down

Top of the bill

THE IDEA THAT DANCE BANDS, besides supplying the essential accompaniment for dancing, could also put on a show that would entertain a more passive audience seems to have occurred to theatre managers shortly after the end of the First World War. When the Original Dixieland Jazz Band arrived from America to play at The Hammersmith Palais, they were also booked to appear at The London Hippodrome in a musical revue called *Joy Bells*. The five young men wore natty dinner jackets and white top hats upon each of which was boldly printed a letter, collectively spelling out the word DIXIE. They played 'The Tiger Rag', written by their trumpet player Nick La Rocca; Emile Christian imitated a tiger on his trombone, Larry Shields wailed defiance on his clarinet, and Tony Sbarbaro, the drummer, added to the general excitement by hitting everything in sight and within easy reach – cowbells, cymbals, woodblock, snare drum, bass drum and tom tom. The Original Dixieland Jazz Band were a great big bouncing hit.

They were so successful that George Robey, the celebrated 'Prime Minister of Mirth', in a gesture more Prime Ministerial than mirthful, and more full of portent than he could possibly have imagined, demanded that 'either they go, or I go.'. As we shall see, the balance of power in such a confrontation was to shift dramatically in later years, but at that time it

Paul Whiteman and his Orchestra in 'Brighter London', with and without the chorus

was no contest. George Robey was the star of the show, and he stayed; the Original Dixieland Jazz Band went.

In March 1923, Paul Whiteman and his Orchestra were booked to appear in a revue called *Brighter London* at the Hippodrome. Whiteman, thirty-three years of age, a former violinist with the Denver Symphony Orchestra, arrived from America with a huge reputation (his recording of 'Whispering' was eventually to log up sales of nearly two million) and the biggest band that had ever been seen. There were fourteen of them, not counting Whiteman and his violin. There was a saxophone section, a brass section, a rhythm section and strings, and they played orchestrations of dazzling complexity, with individual displays of instrumental virtuosity the like of which London had never seen or heard. Whiteman, a portly and dignified personage with an already receding hairline and a segmented Dapper Dan moustache, was to return home, enlarge his orchestra to twenty-four players, and make jazz history with a concert at the Aeolian Hall in New York at which a young composer named George Gershwin performed the piano part of a little orchestral work he called 'Rhapsody In Blue'.

Jack Hylton saw the Whiteman band at the Hippodrome, liked what he saw, and said in effect, that's for me. The following year he was appearing at the Alhambra Theatre in Leicester Square with the band which was to dominate the stages of Britain and those of most of Europe for the next decade. The Hylton band toured for most of the year, creaming off the best of the British dates. When, in December, the pantomime season descended upon the land, they resumed their majestic progress around the capitals of Europe. Paris, Rome, Berlin, Brussels, Milan, Prague, they were welcomed everywhere. In 1930, the grateful French awarded their favourite *vedette Anglaise* a *légion d'honneur*, and in 1932 Jack and his band travelled some thirty thousand miles. The likeness of Jack Hylton, his stocky back turned to the observer, his arms raised in the attitude of conducting, and bearing the caption 'Jack's Back!', was as familiar in Munich as it was in Manchester. Never before had a British band achieved such international celebrity, and it would be the 'sixties and the age of The Beatles before it would happen again.

Another American to appear with his band at the London Hippodrome in the mid-'twenties was Ted Lewis. He wore a battered top hot, a wistfully yearning expression, and he played lousy clarinet. The curtain rose to discover him in a follow spot upon a darkened stage. He gazed up at 'the gods' and sang (or rather talked over the music in the manner later adopted by Rex Harrison in *My Fair Lady*): 'Say, don't you know who I am, with this horn in my hand? Why, I'm that ol' medicine man – for your bloo-oooo-ooze. . . .' He would then enquire, in a voice heavy with concern: 'Is everybody happy?' His audience, already entranced, would agree that they were. Ted Lewis was to return to England in 1933 to play the London Palladium, and he was to horrify the local jazz buffs by bringing with him the great Jimmy Dorsey, who sat in the band and

Two showmen of the clarinet. Above, Ted Lewis and, right, Harry Roy

noodled around the lower register of his clarinet, all but inaudibly, while the 'ol' medicine man' stood out front and wailed and howled through his 'horn' like a soul in torment.

It was now becoming clear to bandleaders, and to those who aspired to that exalted status, that there were in fact two distinctly different kinds of band, the dance band and the show band; that the two were mutually exclusive and that you had better make up your mind which of the two you wanted to lead. If you chose to lead a show band, then you and your musicians were going to need skills and talents that were only remotely connected with the making of music. It was Jack Hylton who was setting the pace and laying down the ground rules for success upon the stage. What you needed was what he had: singers, dancers, comedians, elaborate concert arrangements and grandiose finales. If you wanted to get into the game it was as well to learn something about how the game was played.

Among the first to follow Hylton into the unknown land of black outs, back drops and amber spots was Harry Roy. In 1931 he formed a band to appear at the new RKO Theatre in Leicester Square, whose management was about to launch something they called Non-Stop Variety, a form of

Jack Payne poses on the engine of a special train which will rush him from Chatham to London for a broadcast, and back to Chatham in time for the second house. The year was 1932

employment which turned out to be not unlike a short stint in a Siberian salt mine. Harry Roy was small, dark and volatile, and he had boot button eyes which gave him a touch of the Eddie Cantors. He was a street dancer, the way others are street fighters. He leapt and cavorted in front of his white-jacketed band, played a clarinet that reminded his admirers of Ted Lewis and the Dixieland kings of the 'twenties and his detractors of a cat being dragged backwards through a barbed wire fence. He also sang songs like 'Somebody Stole My Gal' in a high strangulated tenor voice. His band featured the piano duets of Ivor Moreton and Dave Kaye, and the frenetic and reckless drumming of Joe Daniels. Harry Roy and his RKOlians were an immediate and riotous hit, and Roy was embarked upon a career that was to win him all the glittering prizes.

In 1932 Jack Payne, musical director of the official BBC Dance Orchestra, decided that the time had come to cash in on the new fame that had come his way through the magic of radio, and embarked with his band on a tour of the music halls. His stage show set out deliberately to compete for top honours with Jack Hylton, the established master. Payne had an eighteen-piece band, which included Jack Jackson on trumpet, Billy Thorburn and Bob Busby on two pianos, a string section of three violins, and 'Poggie' Pogson among the reeds. There were two male vocalists, Billy Scott Coomber and Ronnie Genarder. Payne specialised in those resolutely cheerful songs that proliferated in 1932–33 and were Tin Pan Alley's contribution to the Depression: 'Smile, Darn Ya, Smile', 'There's A Good Time Coming (be it ever so far away)', and 'Give Yourself A Pat On The Back'. He also displayed a taste for jingoistic one-steps usually involving army uniforms and a fair amount of marching up and down: 'The King's Horses', 'Round The Marble Arch' and 'There's Something About A Soldier'. It was all very jolly, very hearty, and aggressively British. And in those troubled times of brown shirts in Berlin and black shirts in London, ever so faintly sinister.

Another bandleader who took the plunge into Variety at roughly the same time was Billy Cotton. He was a big man, warm and generous by nature, who was almost unique in the band world in that he was quite genuinely loved by the musicians who worked for him (unlike Jack Payne, who was just as heartily loathed). He had a highly developed sense of fun, perfectly reflected in his stage show which was loud, unpretentious, good-natured, undisciplined and extremely funny. The comedy was of the funny hat, rolled-up trousers variety, and was to become the model for stage band comedy for ever after.

Nobody, however, looked remotely likely to challenge the ascendancy of the little maestro himself, Jack Hylton. By 1931 his band had grown to become some twenty strong and is worthy of some detailed attention. On trumpets were Jack Raine and Philippe Brun, on trombones, Paul Fenhoulet and Les Carew. The saxophones, led by Dave Shand, had Abe Romaine and Chappie d'Amato on the other altos and Billy Ternent and

Jack Hylton and his wife Ennis, in Berlin. And, right, meeting the boat that brought Duke Ellington to England in 1933. In the background, Irving Mills, Duke's manager

Johnny Raitz on tenors. The violinists were Johnny Rosen and Maurice Loban; Billy Munn was the pianist, Sonny Farrar played banjo and guitar, Clem Lawton played both brass and string bass, percussion was shared by Neville Bishop and Harry Robbins. (The following year, Hylton would add a third drummer, Gilbert Webster.) The vocalists were Pat O'Malley, Jack Plant and Leslie Sarony, and the band's permanent arranger was Peter Yorke.

The most remarkable thing about the show presented by Jack Hylton and his Band was that the entire repertoire was played without music or music stands. Since it involved memorizing some fifty or sixty scores, many of them with highly complex variations of rhythm and tempi, this was a considerable feat, unmatched by any other band in the world. Besides being first-class musicians, many of the band were talented entertainers, in particular Billy Munn, Sonny Farrar and Johnny Raitz the corner man tenor player, he of the spectacularly mobile eyebrows. And when in 1933 Hylton engaged the services of a German-born saxophone player named Freddie Schweitzer, he had found a real star. Schweitzer was a clown, and a great one. Dave Shand, the lead alto player with the band from 1931–35, remembers him well: 'As I sat next to him on the bandstand, I became the straight man to his clowning; he used to call

me "mein partner". One of his acts was to balance a violin on his forehead while playing a jazz chorus on clarinet. (It was good jazz, too.) I remember one concert in France when someone in the audience shouted something during this act of Freddie's, a remark which drew a roar of laughter from the audience. When he returned to his seat, he was obviously put out. "What did he say?" he asked. I translated for him. "He said, why don't you do it with a bass fiddle?" Sure enough, after a few days' practice, Freddie was balancing the huge bass fiddle on his forehead while playing the same jazz chorus on his clarinet.'

In 1933, Hylton turned impresario and presented Duke Ellington and his Orchestra to a startled and largely disinterested British public; in 1934, the band celebrated its tenth anniversary at the Holborn Empire in London, and in 1940, when the door to Europe had been firmly closed and the armed forces of the realm were picking off his precious front line players one by one, Hylton decided to call it a day and leave the field to the newly famous radio bands.

Famous these bands undoubtedly were, and most of them made better music – slicker, more modern, better rehearsed – than Hylton did; but none of them was to come within a light year of usurping his place as a joyous entertainer, the musician as showman. For when Jack Hylton quit he took the secret with him.

By the mid-'thirties, British music hall, now rechristened 'Variety' to distinguish it from the earlier more indigenous genre, was having something of a struggle to survive. The theatres were still there, mighty Moss Empires with its flagships, the London Palladium and the Holborn Empire, and its branches in every major city; and a couple of hundred lesser halls. They were all open for business. The rank and file of the music hall performers, the acrobats, the jugglers, the magicians and the ventriloquists, the adagio dancers and the paper tearers, were still there and clamouring for attention. But the star, that essential, indispensable top-of-the-bill drawing card, was becoming increasingly hard to find. Stars like Gracie Fields, Will Fyffe, George Robey, Will Hay and Harry Tate were less and less prepared to face the hardships of the provincial tour; from America, Sophie Tucker would pay us an occasional visit, and from Paris, Maurice Chevalier would sometimes honour us with his presence. But there just weren't enough to go round. In an effort to plug the gap, George Black, ruler of the Palladium, put his comedians together in bundles of eight – or even ten. Flanagan and Allan, Nervo and Knox, Naughton and Gold, Billy Caryll and Hylda Mundy became 'The Crazy Gang'; still the demand was not being fully met. And then it was discovered that a band, a dance band, one of the BBC's chosen few, could fill a Variety Theatre with fans eager to see their late-night favourites in the living flesh.

In 1934, Roy Fox, fresh from the Café Anglais and the Café de Paris, took his band on the road. He had five brass, four saxes, and a rhythm section. His singers were the Wagnerian Peggy Dell and a gentle crooner

named Denny Dennis. They played, they sang, they offered the statutory dose of band comedy and they sold every seat in every theatre in every town they visited. The message was clear for all to read: radio bands were the new top of the bill. They and they alone could halt the decline of Variety; they and they alone could keep the doors open and the seats filled. Before long they all wanted their piece of the action. Lew Stone, Jack Jackson, Ambrose, Henry Hall, Joe Loss – they all packed their bags and took to the rails. The halls were alive with the sound of music.

No matter that few if any of the bandleaders were showmen. No matter that they didn't know a proscenium arch from a hole in the wall. All over the country the curtain was rising twice nightly on an invariable bill of fare; the first half of the entertainment was composed of four or five variety acts, followed by the interval, followed by one variety act working in a front cloth (so that the musicians could set up noisily behind), followed by – the band. There they always were in their inevitable white tuxedos, seated on rostra spread across the stage like some happy-go-lucky firing squad, and playing their oh so familiar programme of our-latest-recording-these-you-have-loved broadcast favourites.

93

The Variety artistes, the old pros, the stand-up comics, the dog acts, the farmyard impressionists, the female impersonators, all hotly resented this ill-mannered, not-so-much-as-a-by-your-leave intrusion by amateurs and incompetents into their domain. But what could they do? The bands were pulling them in, and everybody, it was argued, was sharing in their success.

When in 1937 Ambrose, most famous of all the broadcasting bands, finally agreed to accept a month's engagement at the London Palladium, the box office was besieged and the season sold out in record time. When on that first Monday night the band was heard to play the opening bars of its signature tune, 'When Day Is Done', the applause was overwhelming. And when the tabs parted to reveal the band, Ambrose, favourite of kings and princes, was so appalled by the thunderous sound that he continued to stand with his back to the audience, refusing to acknowledge such a

Joe Daniels and his Hot Shots

vulgar display of acclamation. Billy Amstell, the tenor player, hissed out of the side of his mouthpiece: 'Turn around Bert, turn around!' And at last, squinting over his shoulder at his admirers, the maestro offered them a friendly grin. Some showman!

The musicians approached their Variety tours with somewhat mixed feelings. While it made a nice change from the nightly grind of the West End oom-ching circuit, there was the dreary business of having to look for digs in strange provincial towns. And they were chagrined to find themselves blackballed by landladies who knew all about the nasty things musicians got up to in their spare time, and refused to shelter them in their respectable semi-detached guest houses. The musicians enjoyed the applause their music received from appreciative audiences, and although it was a far cry from the hysteria that rock and roll stars were to provoke some twenty years later, they could nevertheless always find a gratifyingly substantial knot of feminine admirers lingering at the stage door.

The big bands continued to top the bill up to and through the war years, and somewhere along the way they produced a progeny of smaller outfits, usually led by an instrumentalist who had outgrown the patronage of a bandleader and reckoned that the time had come to make it on his own. Nat Gonella and his Georgians were one such, and Joe Daniels (formerly the drummer with Harry Roy) and his Hot Shots were another. Ambrose launched a group called The Ambrose Octette, to exploit the talents of Evelyn Dall, his vivacious blonde American singer, Vera Lynn, soon to be the Forces Sweetheart, and Max Bacon.

Lovers of traditional English music hall have often said that the coming of the bands marked the beginning of the end for that venerable institution. But had it not been for the bands, Variety would probably have died many years earlier than it did. Other forces contributed to its decline and fall: the cinema, blazing into Technicolor and stereophonic sound, and television, waiting only for war's end to deliver the *coup de grâce*. It was not the bands that killed the music hall, but the changing times and the desperate last-ditch methods of the managements, who, by 1950, were busily waxing the slippery slope that leads to oblivion by short-changing the customers with tatty shows with names like 'No Nudes Is Good Nudes', and 'Strip, Strip, Hooray!', full of listless girls and foul-mouthed comics.

All that jazz

LEW DAVIS, FOR MANY YEARS THE best jazz trombonist in the land, and indispensable member of the Ambrose, Lew Stone and Ray Noble brass sections, tells the following story. 'In 1920 I was still a schoolboy, but my older brother Ben was already a professional saxophone player in the West End. The band he was with needed a trombone player and there just wasn't one to be had. There were probably no more than three trombonists in the entire country who had the foggiest notion of how to play dance music, and they, it seems, were all working. Ben said, "What about you?" I said, "Who? Me? I hardly know which end of a trombone to blow through let alone how to play it." "What are you?" said big brother Ben. "Some kind of a defeatist? We'll find you a trombone and you'll learn how to play it. Okay?" So we toured the pawn shops and we bought a very nice, only slightly dented tenor trombone and bore it home with us. I said, "How long have I got to learn to play this thing?" "How long can it take?" Ben asked irritably. "All you have to do is yum yum yum, aw yum yum, yumma ta tum tum." So I spent the rest of the afternoon learning the trombone part for three tunes; they all went, yum yum yum, aw yum yum, yumma ta tum tum. And that same night, wearing a borrowed dinner jacket, I was duly launched upon a career as a professional trombone player.'

That's how it was in 1920. Jazz, this new and outlandish way of making dance music, was so strange to British ears that there were few musicians able to master its technique and feeling. The Original Dixieland Jazz Band had played at the Hammersmith Palais, and as is the way with such novelties, it had interested and excited some, but had appalled as many others, just as the sound of rock was to shock and alienate the main stream of jazz musicians in the 'fifties. And one thing was for sure: as far as jazz was concerned, there was only one source of information, one fount of all knowledge, and that was the United States of America. This was American music, and if you wanted to get into it, you had better listen to the way Americans played it.

Bert Ambrose had got it right. As an adventurous youth he had made his own way to the States, and in 1917, at the age of twenty, had become musical director of a place called the Club De Vingt in New York. It was there that Luigi, the legendary Maitre D', found him and persuaded him to return to London to lead his band at The Embassy Club in Bond Street.

For the rest of the musicians, marooned on an island three thousand miles from where the action was, the best they could do was wait for the occasional visitor from that other musical planet, listen and learn. In 1923, Paul Whiteman arrived with his band; fourteen musicians arranged in sections – saxes, brass, rhythm, strings – and playing cleverly orchestrated pieces as an ensemble. Together. As one man! (Listen, listen!) Other bands followed. That same year Paul Specht came to play at Lyons Corner House in Coventry Street, and in 1925 Vincent Lopez appeared at The Kit Cat Club. In 1929 Gus Arnheim and his Orchestra were at the Savoy, and in 1930, Hal Kemp brought a good dance band to the Café de Paris. Listen, listen!

All through the 'twenties things were changing; the music, the musicians, even the instruments. The C Melody saxophone, that old army marching-band veteran, was found to be more suited to the new music if it was pitched in E flat to carry the melody and in B flat to supply the harmony; the combination of two E flat altos and one B flat tenor made an ideal saxophone section. The C Melody was relegated to the hock shop. Incidentally, Frankie Trumbauer, greatest of all the early jazz saxophonists, never made the change. The sousaphone, that sinuous arrangement of gleaming metal which always seemed to be locked in a life and death struggle with its player, was being replaced by the double or contra bass, but without the bow that went with it. Instead that noble orchestral instrument was being picked and slapped to provide the bass underpinning for the rhythm section. Dick Ball was bassist with Ambrose from 1933, and his name onomatopoeically demonstrated how it sounded: Dick Ball, Dick Ball, Dick Ball, D'Ball D'Ball.

Spanish guitars replaced banjos, trumpets replaced cornets, and slowly but surely the violinists were being eased out of their chairs. The Hal Kemp band at the Café de Paris perfectly exemplified the ideal structure

Busier New Year with Ackroyds' smarter Bandwear!

Improves your appearance, saves you money, brings more engagements.

The "Park Lane" MESS JACKET

The "PARK LANE" Jacket, as offered by Ackroyds and worn by Leading Bands of the British Isles, is undoubtedly the best Mess Jacket ever offered to Musicians. Note the prominent lapels, epaulettes, pocket and cuffs, which look extremely effective in contrasting colour to the jacket, and remember these Jackets are available in 20 different colours and combinations of colours. Buttons are all detachable for washing purposes, and are offered in Chromium, Pearl or Brass. Every Jacket is made to measure and washable, therefore perfect smartness and cleanliness are always assured.

PRICE 12/6 EACH

SEND NOW FOR STYLE SHEET giving details of this Jacket together with many other styles and also specially recommended dress-wear accessories. Shade chart, sample material, self-measurement form, etc., all included with style sheet.

Ackroyds

LEEDS BRIDGE, LEEDS

PHONE 24114

Two American bandleaders of the 'thirties: Hal Kemp (above) and Gus Arnheim

Above, The California Ramblers. Adrian Rollini and Fud Livingston (standing 5th and 6th from the left) and Bobby Davis (seated 2nd from the right) came to England to join Elizalde at the Savoy. Below, The Ben Pollack Band, nursery of great jazzmen. At the back, second from the right, Jack Teagarden. Right in the middle, Benny Goodman

and optimum size of a modern dance orchestra: three saxophones, two altos and a tenor; three brass, two trumpets and a trombone; four rhythm, piano, bass, drums and guitar. The Hal Kemp boys were, by the way, first to wear what was soon to become *de rigeur* for the well-dressed bandsman – white dinner jackets. (Look, look!). The Yanks came and went and their recordings arrived in a steady stream. Ben Pollack, Isham Jones, The California Ramblers, Fred Waring's Pennsylvanians, George Olsen, Abe Lyman. Oh, they were good, those bands.

But now something else was happening. Other recordings were arriving, and they were to have the same effect on some musicians that the painting of Picasso and Braque had had upon the artists of Paris some twenty years earlier. It was becoming increasingly clear to these musicians that there were in fact not one, but two kinds of dance music: the music they played nightly to earn their bread, itself being influenced by the influx from the States; and a startlingly different kind of music they were beginning to hear on American records – music by the bands of Red Nichols, Miff Mole, Frankie Trumbauer, Eddie Lang, Joe Venuti and the Dorsey brothers. And as if those weren't enough to set a musician's head to spinning with fresh ideas and new ways of playing, there were, even more astonishingly, the bands of Duke Ellington, Louis Armstrong, Fletcher Henderson, King Oliver and Luis Russell. Slowly it dawned that everything else was dross; that here, my friends, was the real gold. And it was called jazz.

But how to explain the difference? All that can be said is that while some, hearing jazz for the first time, declared it nothing but a meaningless gabble, others, listening, hunched over their gramophones, were shaken as by a revelation. Jazz invaded their hearts and minds like a new religion, complete with its own pantheon of gods.

It was one thing to hear it and to love it; it was quite another to master it. Only a handful did, and immediately were joined together in an élite; a group at once exalted and outcast, poet and pariah both, dedicating their lives to the making of music that only they and a tiny but devoted audience could comprehend and appreciate. As for making a living at it, there was simply no way. The great British public would have none of it. Oh, the noise! And where was the tune? And how could you possibly dance to it? Elizalde at the Savoy, it has already been noted, had been defeated by just such audience hostility.

There were some nightclubs where it was tolerated, one or two where it was even made welcome (invariably the more disreputable of them). And a few jazz records were made, notably by Spike Hughes at Decca. But the sales were so miserably small that few recording companies were keen to waste their money on them.

Who were they, this new jazz brotherhood, the priests and acolytes of this subterranean movement? As far back as 1926 there had been lively interest at the universities. Fred Elizalde and the Quinquaginta Ramblers at Cambridge were doubtless among the founders of the feast. Spike

Hughes, some years later, was another. An extraordinary tenor saxophone player of patrician looks and bearing named Buddy Featherstonehaugh, yet another. And for some reason, the Scots were deciphering the code and learning the secrets. A trumpet player named Duncan Whyte and a guitarist named Allan Ferguson came down from Glasgow, installed themselves at The Nest Club and turned that fetid cellar into the focal point of most of the jazz activity in the capital. Others followed: George Chisholm, unquestionably the best jazz musician Britain ever produced, Tommy McQuater, Andy McDevitt, Benny Winestone, Archie Craig. Jazzmen all.

Here and there, jazz clubs were springing up, havens of adulation housed in the upstairs rooms of pubs and in suburban Town Halls. The jazzers joined in the eagerly arranged jam sessions, but treated their admirers with indifference and some disdain. The making of jazz was always too private an activity to be shared willingly with amateurs, however appreciative.

In 1933 there happened the greatest event so far in the lives of the jazzmen, the appearance at the London Palladium of Duke Ellington and his Famous Orchestra. There they all were, in the flesh! All those marvellous musicians. The jazzmen could name them all: Artie Whetsol, Cootie Williams, Freddie Jenkins, trumpets; Tricky Sam Nanton, Juan Tizol and Lawrence Brown, trombones. Six brass! Johnny Hodges, Otto Hardwicke, Harry Carney, Barney Bigard, saxes. Wellman Braud, bass, Freddie Guy, guitar, Sonny Greer on drums and the Duke on piano. And there were the numbers they all knew by heart, note for note: 'Mood Indigo', 'Rose Room', 'Creole Love Call', 'Sophisticated Lady' (with the incredible Johnny Hodges solo), and 'It Don't Mean A Thing If It Ain't Got That Swing'. The jazzers sat in the stalls night after night and exchanged anguished glances. They moaned and sighed, half in ecstasy, half in torment, wondering whether they would ever learn to play like that.

It was even more shattering when Louis Armstrong and his Hot Five came to England in 1935. The immortal Satchelmouth himself! Armstrong toured the Moss Empires: The Palladium, The Holborn Empire, the Empires at Finsbury Park and Shepherds Bush. The great British public stayed away in their thousands. For the jazzers, the tour became a pilgrimage, and they followed Satchmo from theatre to theatre, often watching and listening marooned in a desert of empty seats. And what were poor jazz-deaf people to make of this glistening, grinning black man with his beautiful shirts cut low on a column of muscled neck which expanded frighteningly when he blew his golden trumpet? And who perspired so copiously that when he turned sharply on stage, the front rows of the stalls were liberally showered with his sweat? The jazzers clung to every great big fat note of every one of the sweetly familiar tunes he played: 'Basin Street Blues', 'Ain't Misbehavin'', 'I'm A Ding Dong Daddy', 'You're Driving Me Crazy', 'Shine'.

LCOME DUKE ELLINGTON!

yet another **Gibson** Triumph!

W OF DUKE ELLINGTON'S ORCHESTRA
GIBSON "6 STRING" GUITAR — ! !

DUKE ELLINGTON'S RHYTHM SECTION.

"GET A GIBSON!"

hat bit of advice has been passed along thousands of
times by America's leading artists and teachers. It is
wise advice. It means complete satisfaction with
the fretted instruments you select. So—get a

Gibson

SEND NOW FOR
CATALOGUES
POST
FREE!

ICIS, DAY & HUNTER, LTD.
usical Instrument Dept., under the
personal supervision of
ALVIN D. KEECH.
HARING X RD., W.C.
one; Tem. Bar
935! 5.

GIBSON PLAYERS ALL!

HARRY SHERMAN
Carroll Gibbons' Savoy Orph.

ALBERT HARRIS
Jack Padbury's Band

GEO. DICKINSON
Henry Hall's B.B.C. Band

BILL TRINGHAM
Late of Bert Ambrose's Blue Lyres

GEO. ELLIOTT
Pas. Troise's Mandoliers

HARRY DAVIES
Astoria Romany Band

BERT THOMAS
Radio and Recording Artist

NICK LUCAS
American Recording Star

ALLAN FERGUSON
Recording Artist

EDDIE HAYES
Godowsky's Orchestra

THE LATE **EDDIE LANG**
—— most Rhythmic of all Guitarists

10

**Duke Ellington and his
Orchestra at the Palladium,
1933**

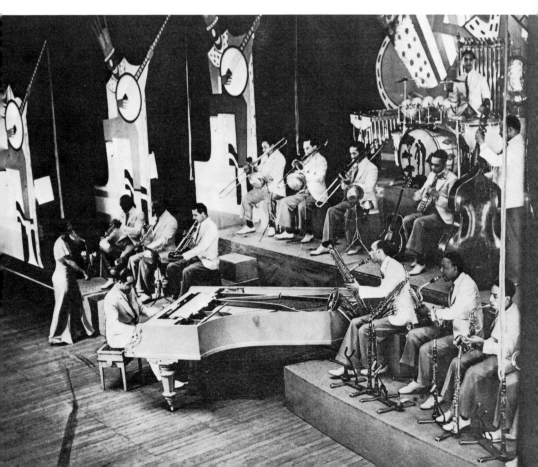

Just because my hair is curly,
Just because my colour's shady;
Just because I always wear a smile,
Like to dress up in the latest style . . .

How strange, with hindsight, to think of that dear man, the one authentic genius in the world of jazz, singing those insulting and fatuous lyrics, 'Uncle Tomming', as someone has said, 'from the heart'; a million miles from Miles.

And how were the British bands responding to all this creative excitement? Well, Elsie Carlisle was wowing 'em on the radio with 'Little Man You've Had A Busy Day', and 'Home James, And Don't Spare The Horses'; songwriters Jimmy Kennedy and Willi Grosz were contributing 'The Isle Of Capri' and 'Red Sails In The Sunset'; everyone was playing and singing 'Smoke Gets In Your Eyes' and 'When I Grow Too Old To Dream'; the crooners were all trying to sound like Bing Crosby singing 'Love In Bloom'; and a cabaret star named Hildegarde was enchanting the supper crowd at the Café de Paris with 'Darling, Je Vous Aime Beaucoup'.

Meanwhile, six thousand miles from London, at the Palomar Ballroom in Hollywood, a clarinet player named Benny Goodman had put together a fourteen-piece band full of good jazz musicians, had persuaded a pianist bandleader named Fletcher Henderson to write some arrangements for it, and had thereby invented a new kind of big band music which would henceforth be known as Swing. As a matter of fact, there wasn't all that much that was new about swing; the black bands, Duke Ellington, Count Basie, Fletcher Henderson, Don Redman and Jimmy Lunceford had been playing that way for years. All Goodman had done was smooth off the rough edges, unkink the hair, remove some of the padding from the shoulders and thereby provoke adolescent America to such a Dionysian frenzy that by 1939, with Artie Shaw, Tommy and Jimmy Dorsey, Charlie Barnet, Woody Herman and Goodman himself leading the dance, swing bands had become a hundred-million-dollar business.

What interested the British musicians as much as all this spectacular success was the realisation that here at last was a kind of dance music that had been fashioned by the musicians themselves out of their own feeling for jazz, and that the new swing bands were being led by the best of their own kind. Benny Goodman, soon to be crowned King of Swing, was a clarinet player of rare talent – Artie Shaw and Jimmy Dorsey, likewise. For the first time, the musicians seemed to be in command of their own destinies. It was, as it happened, not quite so. The tyrant bandleaders had simply been replaced by a new menace, the tyrant manager.

If British musicians were never to see the famous American swing bands, except occasionally in some film starring Alice Faye and Don Ameche, there was no shortage of gramophone records to listen to and to wonder at. Goodman produced a two-sided opus called 'Swing, Swing, Swing', which featured not only his own miraculous clarinet playing, but

Benny Goodman and his band before the famous Palomar Ballroom engagement and his coronation as King of Swing

the exciting drumming of Gene Krupa and the muscular trumpet playing of Harry James. And there were other memorable items – Tommy Dorsey's 'On The Sunny Side Of The Street', Artie Shaw's 'Begin The Beguine', not to mention record after record from Ellington, Basie and Lunceford that dazzled and dismayed the local boys.

The British bandleaders, too, responded to the new sound, but seemed unable to compete with the Americans. The nearest Ambrose came was with a tune called 'The War Dance Of The Wooden Indians'; Lew Stone's contribution was 'The Flat Foot Floogie (With The Floy Floy)'. It wasn't that they weren't trying, but simply that the BBC and the recording companies would raise their hands and cry 'not commercial' any time the bandleaders tried something more adventurous. One brave attempt to bridge the yawning chasm was made in February 1939 by a group of musicians, mostly from an Ambrose band temporarily becalmed, who got together to form a co-operative which they called somewhat clumsily, 'The Heralds Of Swing'. There were ten of them and their avowed policy was to eschew the 'commercial' and play only what pleased them. They

'Jazz Jamborees' began in 1939 and continued annually until they fizzled out in the late 'fifties, defeated by the decline of the big bands and the arrival of the rock 'n' roll groups

were engaged to play at The Paradise, a nightclub in Regent Street with pretensions to classiness and a cabaret which featured Edward Cooper singing 'sophisticated songs' (dirty lyrics), and Desda Kumari, a lady described in the brochure as 'the skating Venus'. The customers were tolerant when the band refused to play waltzes, surly when their tempi proved to be either too fast or too slow to dance to, and aggressive when the open brass drowned their conversation. In May, the management regretted, alas, that the band's services would no longer be required, and by July, The Heralds Of Swing were no more. The *Melody Maker* recorded the event with sadness and a hopelessly mixed metaphor: *Heralds with Clipped Wings*, and mourned, 'So it can't be done in England', and 'The Great Jazz Slump Continues'.

The 'great jazz slump' did indeed continue. It continues to this day. With never more than a precarious toe-hold on these islands, jazz just about survived the swinging 'forties and the rocking 'fifties; even the 'sixties, when the simpler pleasures of Pop all but swept it from the musical map. Astonishingly, young jazzmen continue to appear. Not only young, but good – playing their instruments with more creative confidence than ever before. How many of them make a living at it is a mystery. Nothing, however, seems able to stop them trying.

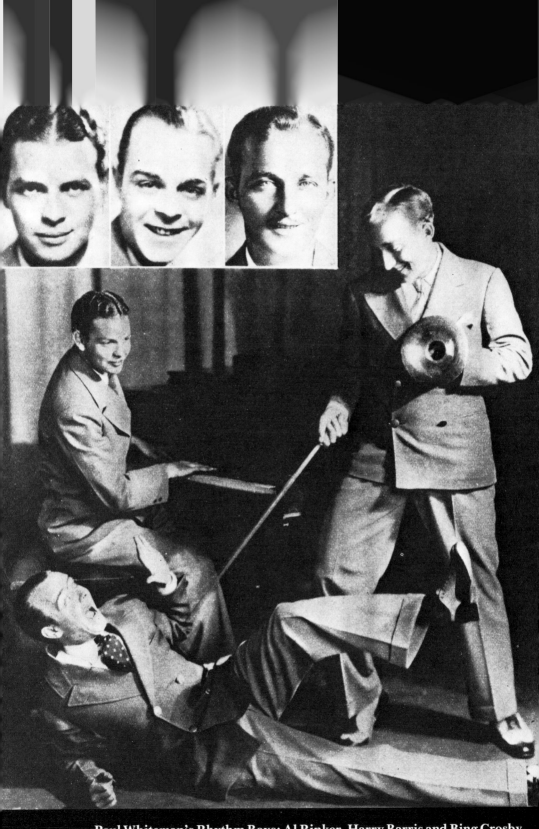

Paul Whiteman's Rhythm Boys: Al Rinker, Harry Barris and Bing Crosby

Learn to croon

> Learn to croon,
> If you want to win your heart's desire,
> Sweet melodies of love inspire
> Romance.
> Just murmur, 'Boo ber boo boo boo',
> And when you do,
> She'll murmur, 'Boo ber boo boo boo',
> And nestle closer to you. . .

Such was the advice offered by Bing Crosby, in a film called *College Humour*, in 1933. And around the world, millions of ardent young men, in front parlours, on park benches and in the back rows of cinemas, were ready and willing to accept it.

The whole business of crooning had started a good deal earlier than that. Way back in 1924, at the Savoy Hotel in London, a violinist named Cyril Ramon Newton was charming the ladies with the words of such songs as 'Felix Kept On Walking', 'Last Night On The Back Porch', and 'Why Did I Kiss That Girl? (Why oh why oh why?)'. While beside him on the Savoy Havana bandstand there sat a young man with the looks of an all-American college boy, who played the alto saxophone, and who the following year would return to his native land, form a band called 'The

Connecticut Yankees', decide to try the singing dodge for himself, and thereby enshrine the word 'crooner' for ever in the English language (*croon,* verb intransitive, make a low singing, humming sound; verb transitive, sing or hum in a low tone; crooner, noun; crooning, adjective and noun). His name was Rudy Vallee.

What Rudy Vallee had realised was that the words of the new popular songs called for a more 'cool', less demonstratively emotional delivery than the old ballads, and that because the vocal chorus must be made to mix seamlessly with the surrounding orchestral sounds when the band was playing for dancing, the voice should be presented as just another musical instrument in the ensemble. To this end he slowed down the ballad singer's impassioned *vibrato,* and carefully did not allow the phrasing to stray too far from the four beats of a bar in common time. In order to project his light tenor voice above the accompaniment of the band, he pressed into service a device formerly used only by football coaches, rowing coxswains and political rabble-rousers – the megaphone. Of course, it was the radio's sensitive microphones, doing away with the necessity to shout in order to make oneself heard above the orchestra, which really wrought the change in singing style; and with the introduction of the microphone and the public address system into dance halls and restaurants, the megaphone went the way of the banjo and the sousaphone, and the transformation was complete. Perry Como, another 'crooner' to have experienced those changes, reports that when the microphone first appeared on the bandstand, he used to sing into it *through* his megaphone, until persuaded that this was no longer necessary.

On records too, the words of the songs were becoming more and more a feature of the band's performance. Although for most of the singers it was an anonymous appearance, his or her identity shrouded by a laconic 'with vocal refrain', there were exceptions. In 1926, Bert Ralton and his Havana Band recorded a number called 'Carolina' with vocal refrain by Harry Shalson, and in 1929 Percival Mackey and his Orchestra recorded a number called 'Ain't Love Hell!' with a singer, later famous, named Cavan O'Connor. A little later, the same band recorded 'When The Lilac Blooms Again', and 'Up In The Clouds', with vocal chorus by a young South African named Al Bowlly. By 1930 the list was growing: Les Allen with Pete Mandell's Dance Orchestra, Dan Donovan with Debroy Somers, Sam Browne with Ray Starita, Val Rosing with Billy Cotton, and Ella Logan with Ambrose.

Before leaving the 'twenties behind us, it would be well to mention an American event of some importance. In 1927, Paul Whiteman heard a singer named Bing Crosby and invited him to join the band as part of a vocal trio (the other two members were Harry Barris and Al Rinker) which he called The Rhythm Boys. English jazz fans of 1930 were to note the début of this young man with his languid gestures and his apparently effortless way of singing when, in the film *The King Of Jazz,* The Rhythm

Oh, listen to the band. Rudy Vallee

Cavan O'Connor and, below,
Tommy Dorsey and his band in
a movie. Buddy Rich is on
drums. And that modest
looking young man behind him
is Frank Sinatra

Boys sang 'When the Blackbirds and the Bluebirds Got Together'. Crosby hung around with his favourite musicians in the Whiteman band – Frankie Trumbauer, Eddie Lang, Joe Venuti, and Bix Beiderbecke; he knew and idolized Louis Armstrong, admired all jazz men, and could conceive of no greater joy than to be counted among their number. Listening to Bing on the recording he made in 1932 of 'Some Of These Days', with Trumbauer and Lang behind him, and hearing his 'scat' singing, a wordless way of imitating a jazz musician improvising a hot chorus, you can hear him express all his aspirations.

By then he had outgrown both The Rhythm Boys and the Whiteman band. Whisked off to Hollywood to help feed the new talking monster, he made *The Big Broadcast* in which he sang 'Please' and 'The Blue Of The Night', and thereby initiated one of the most distinguished careers in show business history. Crosby's jazz orientation has been the mainspring of his singing style throughout his long professional life; it accounts for his impeccable phrasing, his perfect intonation (it is doubtful if Bing ever sang an out of tune note in public) and his superb all-round musicianship. Some years after *The Big Broadcast*, in 1940, the same pattern of training and experience was to manifest itself when Frank Sinatra made himself known to the dance music world with Tommy Dorsey's band. Sinatra confirms this on his 1965 commemorative album 'A Man And His Music': 'And what did I learn from T-Bone Dorsey? Well, just about everything I know about phrasing and breath control; in fact, I may be the only singer who ever took vocal lessons from a trombone. Old T.D. could blow that thing a whole week on just one tank of air, and I latched on to his secret.'

There were plenty of crooners in Britain in those early 'thirties, but alas, no Crosbys. The band singer of that time was likely to be one of the musicians who had either volunteered for the job or been press-ganged into it by his boss. Occasionally it was the bandleader himself. Sometimes the crooner was a non-instrumentalist who sat with the band's front line, self-consciously pretending to play a guitar (equipped with rubber strings); and the ladies, who began to appear on bandstands around 1931, merely sat there, hands folded demurely in satin-clad laps, until such time as their services were required at the microphone.

A favourite crooner of the early 'thirties was Jack Plant. Between 1930 and 1936 he sang with the bands of Pete Mandell, Hal Swain, Roy Fox, Bertini, Teddy Joyce and Sidney Kyte. In 1931, Elsie Carlisle, the first of the girl singers to make an impression, was singing with Jack Payne, joining Ambrose the following year to begin her long and successful partnership with Sam Browne. In 1932, among the crooners regularly recording and broadcasting were Al Bowlly, Cavan O'Connor, Les Allen, Dan Donovan, The Carlisle Cousins (not cousins of Elsie), Jack Plant, Sam Browne, The Three Ginx, Anona Winn, Peggy Dell, Ronnie Genarder, Val Rosing, Alan Breeze, Sam Costa, Peggy Cochrane, and Billy Scott-Coomber.

Not everybody welcomed the crooners (or vocalists as they now preferred to be called) with open ears; some positively loathed the sight and sound of them. Beverley Nichols, in his book *The Sweet And Twenties,* was moved to anathematize them thus: 'One of the few times I feel very old – and very angry – is when I hear a modern crooner murdering rhythm. There he stands, in front of the microphone, with his pygmy voice and his drooling lips and his over-sexed uvula, singing a blues number which is a rhythmic nightmare. Sudden breathless *accelerandos* – sudden inexplicable *rallentandos* – sudden gulps and pauses – the voice and the orchestra in a lunatic conflict.' Difficult to imagine what an 'over-sexed uvula' looks like, or indeed, how close he had to get to spot it between a pair of 'drooling lips', but Mr Nichols makes his point – he can't stand crooners.

He fails, however, to draw attention to the main cause for anger directed against the band singers; it was their infuriating use of an American accent. By 1935, with Bing Crosby selling more copies of his records than anyone else ever had, plus the deluge of American popular songs swamping the British market, boys from Kentish Town were beginning to sound like New York taxi drivers, and lads from Castleford like Mississippi field hands. The fact of the matter was that the songs just didn't sound right unless the lyrics were sung with an American accent. For one thing, unless the short 'A' was used, nothing rhymed: 'May I have the next romance with you? Do I stand harf a charnce with you?' Added to which, the words often sounded all wrong with an English accent. When BBC announcers, with their mouths full of aniseed balls, said: 'And for their next number the band will play, "It doesn't mean a thing if it hasn't got that swing",' well, the boys in the band just fell about. Jack Payne was one who resisted Americanization. When he sang with his band, as he frequently did, it was in a hoarse tenor voice and with a defiant golf-club English accent, clearly proclaiming that he at least was not to be seduced by the unspeakable Yankees. Denny Dennis, a good vocalist who sang with Jack Jackson in 1933, and subsequently with Roy Fox and Ambrose, made no bones about it. He proclaimed himself the 'English Bing Crosby', developed a singing style that was remarkably like his idol's and nobody minded a bit.

By 1937, the band singers were firmly established as an essential part of the dance music scene. Their importance on the bandstand, on records and on the air was more and more apparent; the first faint glimmerings of stardom were to be seen. Sam Costa was with Lew Stone, Vera Lynn and Evelyn Dall were with Ambrose. Jack Cooper and Helen Clare were with Jack Jackson, Bruce Trent and Peggy Dell with Jack Hylton. And Al Bowlly, newly returned from his years in America with Ray Noble, was singing with practically everybody.

Al Bowlly was unquestionably the closest the British ever came to producing a singing star of the stature of Crosby or Sinatra. He arrived in England from South Africa, via the Far East and Germany, and is first heard of in Britain singing with Fred Elizalde in 1928. In 1932, broadcasting and recording with Lew Stone and the Monseigneur Band made him

Sherriffs draws the crooners. Extreme left, Joe Crossman; top row (left to right) Brian Lawrence, Elsie Carlisle and Sam Costa; middle row, Gerrie Fitzgerald, Les Allen, Harry Bentley and George Barclay; front row, Sam Browne, Harry Roy (with sax), Peggy Dell, Nat Gonella (with trumpet), and Phyllis Robbins; Girvan Douglas stands behind the microphone; extreme right, Peggy Cochrane

Band singers: Evelyn Dall with Ambrose (above left); Al Bowlly with Lew Stone (above right); and Ella Fitzgerald with Chick Webb

the most popular singer in the land, and his additional recording with Ray Noble at HMV made him the busiest. It was those latter recordings and the popularity they had achieved in the United States which had led to his engagement with Ray Noble, late in 1934, at the Rainbow Room on top of the RCA Building, Radio City, New York. Noble's American band had been put together for him by a trombonist arranger named Glenn Miller, and included, besides Miller himself, such celebrated musicians as Charlie Spivak and PeeWee Erwin on trumpets, Bud Freeman and Johnny Mince on saxophones, Claude Thornhill, piano, George Van Epps, guitar, and Delmar Kaplan on bass. The drummer was Bill Harty, the only British instrumentalist the American Federation of Musicians would allow.

It is sad that Al Bowlly should have exchanged his enormous popularity in Britain for the chance of an American career, at just the moment when the interest was shifting from the comparatively commercial bands like Noble's to the new, more exciting swing bands of Goodman and Artie Shaw. A glance at the competition which was around in 1937 will give some idea of what Al found himself up against in the States. Dick Haymes and Helen Forrest were with Harry James. Peggy Lee was with Benny Goodman, Perry Como with Ted Weems, Doris Day with Les Brown, Ella Fitzgerald with Chick Webb, and Frank Sinatra and Jo Stafford with Tommy Dorsey! In December of that year Al Bowlly returned to England, licking his wounds. He should, he told himself, have stayed at home.

He never really re-established himself. The bandleaders seemed pleased to have him back, and he immediately returned to work for his old boss, Lew Stone; also for Sydney Lipton, Oscar Rabin, Bram Martin, Geraldo and Maurice Winnick. But the public found other singers to applaud in those years astride the outbreak of war. There was, in particular, the skinny kid who sang 'I'll Never Smile Again' and 'I'll Be Seeing You' on the Tommy Dorsey records and who, a little later on, would have the bobbysoxers screaming and weeping in the aisles of the Paramount Theatre in New York, when he began his remarkable career as an entertainer, and initiated the new era of the singer as superstar. From 1942 through the mid-'fifties, the singers who had learnt their business in the bands would rule the roost: Frank Sinatra, Perry Como, Dick Haymes, Billy Eckstine, Johnny Desmond. And the ladies – Peggy Lee, Doris Day, Ella Fitzgerald, Sarah Vaughan (the Divine Sarah), Betty Hutton, Lena Horne, and the immortal Lady Day herself, who had sung for a brief while with Artie Shaw, Billie Holiday.

In Britain too, the band singers were beginning to make it big; Anne Shelton, Alma Cogan and Vera Lynn were names that were creeping up in the billing. Al Bowlly had crossed the Atlantic only to miss the boat.

Wartime jitterbugs at the Paramount, Tottenham Court Road

'What did you do in the war, daddy?'

WING COMMANDER R. P. O'DONNELL, MVO, Director of Music to the Royal Air Force, had a dream. It was that some day there would be strings seated alongside his brass, woodwind and percussion, and that he would be standing there in front of them, conducting not a military band, but a real symphony orchestra. Now, in September 1939, the fortunes of war were promising to turn the dream into reality. For among the young men who were liable to call-up into the armed services, there were hundreds of musicians anxiously wondering what on earth was to become of them. String players in particular knew with absolute certainty that if ever they were ordered to exchange their instruments for rifles, for even a few months (and who knew how long the war might last?), their playing careers would be over.

O'Donnell let it be known that the RAF would be happy to consider engaging the services of a number of them for the duration of the hos- tilities, and the response was gratifying. From the London Symphony Orchestra, from the Royal Philharmonic, from the Hallé, from the BBC, came violinists, cellists, viola players, double bassists; in no time at all there began to assemble at the RAF Depot at Uxbridge a string section of rare quality. O'Donnell was ecstatic. He had his symphony orchestra. But why stop there? Let's have some dance music as well. At times like these, nothing is too good for our lads in airforce blue. The dance musicians were recruited in their hundreds. The objective: to form them into five-piece bands and disperse them among the RAF stations up and down the country. Their rank: aircraftsman second class/general duties, the lowest of the low, the coolies of the service. Their pay: three and sixpence a day, with bed and board (the beds at Uxbridge, they discovered, were indeed boards). The regulars greeted their arrival with wry amusement: 'Wo ho, the snake charmers!' They stood around the parade ground in their stiff new uniforms and asked themselves what nice boys like them were doing in a place like that.

Set apart from these musicians, if not by airforce rank (they were erks to a man) then by a certain professional glamour, were the fourteen men selected to form an official RAF Dance Orchestra – the band that was to become known as the Squadronaires. Some of them had been with Ambrose at the Mayfair when Rudy O'Donnell's siren song had been heard; all of them had played in big time West End bands. They were told that they would go immediately to France to play for the men who were fighting the war, but that was not to be. By the time they had finished their basic training, France had fallen and there was nothing to do but return to Uxbridge and await what would happen next. What did happen was something quite remarkable. Left with little to do and nothing to spend but time, the Squadronaires rehearsed, experimented, rehearsed some

The Dance Band of the Royal Air Force. The name 'Squadronaires', the invention of the band itself, was never officially approved

more, and soon turned themselves into what was without a doubt the finest swing band ever to be heard outside America. Left to their own devices and freed from the commercial duress their civilian counterparts were subject to – the demands of the dancers, the caution of the recording companies and the rapacity of bandleaders – they were at last able to exploit and develop the creative ideas that musicians had been waiting so long to express.

The call-up continued to ravage the famous bands and the musicians found themselves in one or another of the services. The Royal Army Ordnance Corps had a band called The Blue Rockets, led at first by Eric Robinson and later by trombonist Eric Tann; and the Royal Navy had The Blue Mariners, a band led by pianist George Crow and including among its members Ray Noble's favourite alto player, Freddie Gardner, of the gorgeous tone. There was another outstanding band in the RAF, The Number One Balloon Centre Dance Orchestra. They called themselves The Skyrockets, and can you blame them? Their leader was Paul Fenhoulet, trombonist and fine arranger, and they could count among their numbers such stars as Les Lambert and Chick Smith on trumpets; Don Macaffer, trombone, Izzy Duman and Pat Smuts, saxes; Pat Dodd, piano, Jock Reid, bass, and George Fierstone, an old Heralds Of Swing man, on drums.

In 1939, when Britain had gone to war, the West End had held its

The Skyrockets. Paul Fenhoulet leading on trombone

A London nightclub in 1941. The band are on the shelf

breath. Fearful of what might lie ahead, the hotels had put up their black-out curtains, taped their windows, sandbagged their portals, and waited. Nothing happened. And so, quickly regaining their former aplomb, they declared business as usual, and the customers returned. These customers were the same young men, bouncing on the balls of their feet, out of time with the music, but now they were subalterns, pilot officers and sub-lieutenants; a girlfriend could now gaze at the band over one lonely pip on her partner's shoulder.

The public's appetite for entertainment seemed suddenly to have become insatiable. Cinemas and theatres were jammed for every performance. It was said of Variety that you could fill the house with three Chinese plate jugglers and a dog act – not quite true, but the bandleaders received the message and got themselves and their bands out on to the road for a quick killing. The West End managers received a message of their own: they no longer needed the big-time bandleaders. With a seven-piece band of Grade D rejects, too old or too feeble for the armed forces, oom chinging away up in the corner of the restaurant, they were turning customers away. Who needed Bert Ambrose?

Even the Blitz did nothing to dampen the spirits of people who would never, it seemed, run short of excuses for a night on the town. Mad to celebrate this or that – a call-up, a promotion, an unexpected week-end pass, or a hasty marriage – they groped their way through the black-out to the Savoy and the Café de Paris ('The best air-raid shelter in town, old boy'), and enjoyed the added thrill of dancing the night away while anti-aircraft guns thudded away outside, and the musicians wondered how the hell they were going to get home and what they would find there when they did.

In March 1941, the Café de Paris received a direct hit from a bomb which landed neatly in front of the bandstand. It killed the bandleader, Ken Johnson, a tenor player named Dave Williams, and more than a hundred of the guests. The West End paused for a moment of horrified silence – then the dance went on. A month later Al Bowlly, his career in the doldrums, was in bed in his little flat in Jermyn Street when the blast from a land mine blew his bedroom door in on top of him and killed him instantly. Hardly anyone noted his passing.

In America, the dance band era had arrived at its apogee. In 1940 there were no less than two hundred bands all working full-time. One in particular was causing a stir, not only at home but across the Atlantic as well. It was the band of Glenn Miller. Miller had first put a band together in 1937, but it was 1939 before he was to make his presence felt. In that year he had recorded his theme song, 'Moonlight Serenade', and 'Little Brown Jug'. He followed these with 'In The Mood' and shot himself and his band to stardom. In most respects, Glenn Miller's was another in the direct line of swing bands which had begun with Benny Goodman, but it had some unique features. In 1939, he added a trumpet and a trombone to his three trumpets and three trombones, thus becoming the first of the big bands to use a section of eight brass players. Another feature was the piquant tone colour he was achieving with his saxophone section by doubling the lead alto part with clarinet in the upper register – the Miller sound. And something else. Miller had started with a two-beat band – that is, it drew its rhythmic inspiration from the classical Dixieland style and the relaxed, heavy off-beat playing of bands like the much-admired Jimmie Lunceford's. But he had become more and more attracted by the playing of Count Basie's band, and its impeccable four in the bar rhythm section – by common consent, the best that ever was. Miller pushed the four beat mode to its limits, and upon this ordered and imperturbable framework he superimposed long *legatissimo* phrases, economically and unfussily scored, and played with impeccable precision. The result was both bland and discreetly exciting – dance music which expressed to perfection the new romanticism of the day; the sense of time running out, the poignancy of lovers parting. 'Don't sit under the apple tree with anyone else but me, anyone else but me, anyone else but me, no no no!'

For it was now 1942. America was in the war, and the draft was carrying its young men away just as the call-up had done in Britain in 1939. In September, when he was the leader of the most famous band in dance band history, Glenn Miller gave it all up and joined the army.

Here at home, the Squadronaires had settled down to a ceaseless routine of troop shows and dances which took them all over the country, to Bomber Command, Fighter Command, Coastal Command, Training Command. In and out the counties, up and down the shires. Personnel

Above, Glenn Miller and his famous Orchestra, Hollywood 1941.
Below, Allies. Glenn Miller with Joe Loss and Vera Lynn, England 1944

Glenn Miller and his Army Air Force Band play at Yale University in 1943 . . . and in 1976, the Million Airs play a concert. Glenn Miller lives!

changed little during the war years. The band was led by Jimmy Miller, a Scot from Aberdeen, who, with his brother Billy, had once been piano and violin *enfants prodigieux* with Jack Hylton's stage show. The saxophones were Tommy Bradbury, Monty Levy, Jimmy Durrant, Andy McDevitt and Cliff Townshend; the brass were Tommy McQuater, Archie Craig, Clinton (Froggy) Ffrench, trumpets and Eric Breeze and George Chisholm, trombones; the rhythm section were Ronnie Aldrich, piano, Jock Cummings, drums, Arthur Maden, bass, and this author, who played guitar.

Most of their work took the form of concerts performed for as many airmen, soldiers or factory workers as could be crammed into a hangar, a Naafi, or a works canteen. Concerts were preferred to dances on remote airforce bases mainly because there were never enough women around to provide partners. The Squads' stage show was a standard mix of big band arrangements, instrumental features, popular songs and comedy routines. For the latter, George Chisholm was persuaded, much against his inclination, to uncover a talent for clowning which turned out to be every bit as remarkable as his trombone playing and arranging. The tours were a tough schedule of one-night stands which turned into a nightmare of interminable journeys over non-existent roads in an old down-at-axle Bedford motor coach, of sleep snatched on barrack-room floors, of endless encounters with hopelessly out-of-tune pianos, rickety stages, and public address systems that refused to function, or when they did, howled piteously whenever approached. They called it 'The Grapes of Wrath, With Music.'

The work the Squadronaires enjoyed least was playing for Officers' Mess dances. These were occasions compounded of equal parts command performance and a night on the chain gang. On one such evening the band had been playing for a solid three hours (oom ching, oom ching, just like the Mayfair), and decided to do what big bands usually do in like circumstances. They split up so that half the band could take a well-earned rest without interrupting the steady supply of dance music. Almost immediately, the Commanding Officer, an exalted personage with braid almost up to his uniformed armpits, paused with his lady in front of the depleted bandstand. 'Where is the rest of the band?' he demanded to know. 'Taking a break, sir', politely explained Miller, J., sergeant (acting). The CO began to tremble violently and turn an even darker shade of puce. 'Who gave such an order?' he bellowed. 'I want the full band back on the bandstand, and at the double. Is that clear, sergeant?' It was, and the missing musicians were herded back to work. 'Right,' said the band, in vengeful mood. 'If the full band is what he wants, the full band is what he is going to get!' Whereupon they put up their biggest arrangements, the brass section removed their mutes, and for the rest of the night the Squadronaires proceeded to rattle the walls and shatter the glasswear with the loudest big band music this side of the Savoy Ballroom in Harlem.

126

Vera Lynn, the 'Sweetheart of the Forces', with naval escort

In the Spring of 1944, Glenn Miller arrived in England, and so did the German buzz bombs. Miller's Army Air Force Band was enormous. He had ten brass, including a french horn, six saxes, two drummers, two bassists, two pianists, a guitarist, three arrangers and a copyist. And twenty strings. It wasn't quite the wonderfully smooth machine that the civilian band of 'A String Of Pearls', 'Tuxedo Junction' and 'Kalamazoo' had been, but with such players as drummer Ray McKinley, clarinettist Peanuts Hucko, Tommy Dorsey guitarist Carmen Mastren, and a good singer named Johnny Desmond (known to one and all as The Creamer), it was still a formidable outfit, marked as before by the ruthless efficiency of Glenn Miller. Their principal purpose was of course to entertain their compatriots overseas, but the band broadcast continuously both for the BBC and the American Forces Network, and the British listeners loved every minute of it.

One more American band was to visit Britain before war's end. It was the band of the US Navy, led by Sam Donohue. This was the band put

The meek and the mighty. Sergeant Cyril Hellier and an R.A.F. band; Major Glenn Miller and the band of the AAF

together by Artie Shaw three years earlier, which he had left behind him when ill-health had ended his services career. And what a band it was. When the Squadronaires first heard them, occupying the opposite bandstand for a two-band session at the Queensbury Club in 1945, they felt as if they'd been hit by a truck. This was powerhouse big band stuff, and it made the Squads' elegant George Chisholm arrangements, with their filigreed phrases and virtuoso playing, sound effete and fussily old-fashioned. There was, apart from the awesome grandeur of the ensemble, the matter of sheer volume of sound. The Squadronaires had always thought of themselves as a *loud* band (to produce a double *forte* without sacrifice of intonation and precision was one of the glories of big band playing), but these American matelots were something else. So this, thought the Squads, when their ears had stopped ringing, is what has been happening to our music while our backs have been turned!

Little did they know that within a very few years, four Liverpudlian juveniles with funny haircuts, playing three guitars (one of them back to front) and drums, and aided and abetted by a thousand pounds worth of sophisticated amplification, would be able to produce more decibels than they and the US Navy Band combined were capable of, and would thus put paid to those beautiful big bands for ever.

The road to nowhere

WHEN THE WAR WAS OVER AND Johnny came marching home, some of the services bands decided to stay together; in particular, the RAF's Squadronaires and Skyrockets. The problem they had to face was where to work. When they looked around the West End, at their old comfortable jobs, they saw a desert. The hotels, the restaurants and the smart clubs regarded them with stony-faced disinterest. They had managed very well for the duration without big expensive name bands, and they could think of no good reason for turning the clock back. The orchestra pit at the London Palladium opened up, and the Skyrockets disappeared into it. They did some valiant work there, and they were probably the best pit orchestra the Palladium ever had – but they had ceased to be a dance band.

The Squadronaires got themselves a summer season job and did a bit of recording and broadcasting; but for most of the year they were stuck with one-night stands. And if the old weekly Variety tours had been drudgery, the dreaded one-nighters were the new exile. It was into the coach and drive three hundred miles to a town, set up, grab a meal, find digs, play the gig, go to bed, get up, get back in the coach, and drive two hundred miles to a new town that looked exactly like the one you'd just left. Life was a nightmare of flat tyres, bed bugs and missing laundry; and happiness was a town where they were showing a movie you hadn't seen at least four times before. To the Squads it was all too familiar – it was the Grapes of Wrath with music all over again.

The Americans were faring no better. Glenn Miller had not come marching home. He was lost one dreadful night in December 1944, when his light plane had disappeared into the English Channel. The AAF Band had soldiered on under Ray McKinley, but the Major's death had signalled the end of something. In 1946, Benny Goodman, Woody Herman, Harry James, Tommy Dorsey, Les Brown, Jack Teagarden and Benny Carter all disbanded. The cold winds of post-war austerity were blowing across the land and the lovely lavish eighteen-piece bands were a luxury nobody could afford. The era of the big bands was drawing to a close.

Britain was to witness one magnificent late flowering of big band music when Ted Heath put a band together towards the end of 1945. Heath, a big-time trombonist, an Ambrose and Ray Noble alumnus, chose his personnel from among the musicians returning from the war. It would be, he had decided, a band totally committed to all that had been learned in the preceding years about modern dance music; hard driving, jazz orientated swing that would utilize without compromise the new skills that home-grown musicians had at last thoroughly mastered. They broadcast, recorded, and played a long series of memorable Sunday concerts at the Palladium. An early Ted Heath band included Kenny Baker, Dave Wilkins, Stan Roderick and Alan Franks, trumpets; Harry Roche, Jack Bentley, Laddie Busby and Jimmy Coombes, trombones; Les Gilbert, Reg Owen, Johnny Gray and Henry McKenzie, saxophones; Jack Parnell, drums, Charlie Short, bass, Dave Goldberg, guitar, and Ralph Dollimore, piano. Ted Heath and his Music was the best of the British swing bands – and the last.

By the mid-'fifties, the old maestri were giving up the unequal struggle; Lew Stone was either conducting theatre orchestras or leading inferior bands in down-market rooms like The Pigalle in Piccadilly. Jack Hylton had been an impresario since the war; he was powerful, ruthless and successful and the carefree band days were a fading memory. Jack Jackson was a disc jockey, and Max Bacon was a stand-up comic.

Ambrose was on the road, traipsing around the provinces on a dreary odyssey of one-night stands, trying to stretch some last mileage out of his soon to be abandoned career. The old stalwarts, Max Goldberg, Ted Heath, Danny Pola, Bert Barnes, the archetypal Ambrose bandsmen, were scattered to the winds, gone their separate ways. His band was now a gang of nondescript Archer Street layabouts; unkempt, pot-smoking and profane ruffians who hadn't been born when the great man had been lording it over the gentry at the Embassy Club and the Sporting Club in Monte Carlo. They thought him an old has-been, a square peg in a world where the word 'square' had become the ultimate term of rejection. They made fun of him behind his back, and he tolerated their impertinence for just as long as he could. Then one night, in some nameless Northern town, on the eve of yet another miserable musical evening, he faced them all in the band room and delivered his valediction. 'You fellows think I'm a berk, don't you?' he said. The boys in the band stared at him, not knowing how to respond. 'It's perfectly all right,' said Ambrose. 'I just wanted you to know that I *know* that you think I'm a berk.'

Ted Heath's contribution apart, popular music looked tired and dispirited at war's end. Tin Pan Alley was offering returning-soldier songs: 'It's Been A Long Long Time', and 'A Little On The Lonely Side'. In 1946, the hit song on both sides of the Atlantic was something by a British composer named Billy Reid called 'The Gypsy'. 'In a quaint caravan – there's a lady they call – the gypsy . . .' But her crystal ball told little about the future. All the creative energy seemed to be flowing back to its source – to jazz. And in jazz, momentous things were happening.

In America, an alto saxophone player named Charlie Parker and a master trumpeter named Dizzie Gillespie were busily changing the shape and texture of their music. What they played was delighting the cognoscenti and mystifying the hoi-polloi. It was called be-bop. The story goes that Charlie Parker (the legendary Bird), Dizzy Gillespie, Don Byas, Max Roach, Thelonius Monk, Miles Davis and others invented bop in order to discourage the amateur drummers, tyro horn players and such from sitting in with the band, since 'sitting in' was still the convention in New York's Fifty-second Street clubs like The Onyx, which is where they worked. There may be just a grain of truth in that. It is certainly true that nothing can make a good jazz musician as unhappy as the presence on the bandstand of some fumble-fingered pianist, wrong-chord guitarist, or a drummer who keeps losing the beat. It is also true that the complicated harmonic progressions in bop, and the improvisations which seemed to have nothing whatever to do with the good old familiar common chords, so intimidated the would-be sitters-in that they just stayed at their bandside tables, rattled the ice in their bourbon and dry gingers, and kept quiet. A simpler explanation would be that Bird and Dizzy were making discoveries about their music which could only be shared with other like-minded instrumentalists. Jazz musicians have always been uneasy with an audience, like lovers suddenly aware that their conversation is being overheard. Now, at last, they had achieved the privacy they had always secretly desired. The unwritten, unsung lyrics of be-bop said, 'Look, we don't actually mind you being there – just don't expect us to smile and wave.'

When a popular music form becomes so turned in upon itself that it can no longer be truly popular, the times are ripe for change. The change came around 1955, in the shape of Bill Haley, a chubby American with a slick of damp hair who played country guitar and led a six-piece band which he called his Comets. There was a honking tenor player, a thumping two-beat drummer, and a bass player who lay down on the stage and played his instrument like a shipwrecked sailor adrift on a floating spar. The music they played was crude; the melody nursery-rhyme simple, the

**Bill Haley and the Comets in
1957; more recently, weary
but undaunted, Stan Kenton**

three-chord harmonies a throwback to the earliest days of Dixieland and the ukulele strummers of the 'twenties. They called it rock and roll. 'One two three o'clock, four o'clock rock – five six seven o'clock, eight o'clock rock – nine ten eleven o'clock, twelve o'clock rock, we're gonna rock! around! the clock! tonight . . .'

The musicians were appalled, but Bill Haley's rock and roll sold a zillion records. You could hear the beat (oh, how you could hear the beat!) and it was fun to dance to. And it was something new. There was a whole new public for it, too. They were the evacuees and the blitz babies, who were growing up in a wonderful world of welfare and full employment. They had the money in their pockets to pay their own pipers, and they had the power to call their own tunes. The dance band musicians were rudely elbowed aside. Many of them were too old to learn the new tunes – many more were not, but wouldn't. They found them contemptible. They disappeared quietly into recording studios, where, in the 'sixties, they could be found blowing four-bar fanfares plugging dog food on commercial television.

It remains to spare a thought for the gallant survivors; the big American bands who roam the world in search of an audience. Stan Kenton, Count Basie, Woody Herman, Buddy Rich, and until his death, Duke Ellington, the noblest roamer of them all. The people who attend their concerts in London, Paris and Berlin are mostly the old crowd come to listen and applaud, and hope to hear their favourite numbers – 'One O'clock Jump', 'Take The "A" Train', 'Peanut Vendor', 'Jumping At The Woodside'. They are maudlin with nostalgia. They sit there picking over the past like a jilted bride among the dust and mothballs of her trousseau.

One constantly hears talk these days about a dance band revival. Well of course there isn't one. Nor could there be. And if there could be one, who would want it? The Glenn Miller necrophiliacs notwithstanding, those days are over. They are long gone and good riddance. Because if you are pining for those happy halcyon dance band days of the 'twenties, 'thirties and 'forties, it is well to remember what they were the musical accompaniment to. A lacerating economic depression, a second world war and the Nazi holocaust. May none of them ever return.

Select discography

Original Dixieland Jazz Band (Americans Play Their London Sides) WRC SH 220

The Carroll Gibbons Story (2 LPs) WRC SH 167/8

The Savoy Bands (Havana and Orpheans) (2 LPs) WRC SH 165/6

The Bert Firman Bands (1925–31) (2 LPs) WRC SHB 30

The Sweetest Music This Side of Heaven Maurice Winnick WRC SH 225

Hello Ladies and Gentlemen: Roy Fox Speaking (at the Monseigneur) Decca ACL 1172

The Bands That Matter: Roy Fox Decca ECM 2045

The Bands That Matter: Lew Stone Decca ECM 2047

The Bands That Matter: Ambrose Decca ECM 2044

Ambrose Plays Cole Porter Decca ACL 1186

Make Those People Sway The Jack Jackson Orchestra WRC SH 210

The Jack Harris Orchestra (1937–39) WRC SH 219

Geraldo WRC SH 215

Say It With Music Jack Payne Decca ECM 2111

Henry Hall and the BBC Dance Orchestra WRC SH 140

Dance Bands on the Air: Weekend Sounds Series, Vol. 1 BBC REC 139

Dance Bands on the Air: Weekend Sounds Series, Vol. 2 BBC REC 140

Ten-thirty Tuesday Night: Lew Stone with Al Bowlly and Nat Gonella Decca ACL 1147

The Ray Noble Orchestra with Al Bowlly 1935–36 (The Radio Years) London HMG 5019

They Called Me Al Al Bowlly Decca ECM 2048

Al Bowlly with Lew Stone and His Band Decca ACL 1178

Making Whoopee to the Music of Walter Donaldson (Hylton, Ambrose, Savoy Orpheans, Firman) WRC SH 229

The Bands That Matter: Jack Hylton Decca ECM 2046

The Band That Jack Built: Jack Hylton, 1935–39 WRC SH 190

Jack Hylton and his Orchestra WRC SH 127

Billy Cotton and his Band WRC SH 141

The World of Harry Roy The Harry Roy Orchestra Decca SPA 141

The Golden Age of British Dance Bands (2 LPs) WRC SH 165/6

Bands on Film (Harry Roy and Nat Gonella) WRC SH 197

London Jazz Scene: the '40s Decca ACL 1121

There's Something in the Air Squadronaires Decca ECM 2112

This is Glenn Miller and the Army Air Force Band (2 LPs) RCA DHY 0004

Big Band World of Ted Heath Decca SPA 514

LAMBERT & BUTLER'S CIGARETTES

AMBROSE

LAMBERT & BUTLER'S CIGARETTES

BILLY COTTON

LAMBERT & BUTLER'S CIGARETTES

DUKE ELLINGTON

LAMBERT & BUTLER'S CIG

ROY FOX

LAMBERT & BUTLER'S CIGARETTES

JACK HYLTON

LAMBERT & BUTLER'S CIGARETTES

JACK JACKSON

LAMBERT & BUTLER'S CIGARETTES

CHARLIE KUNZ

LAMBERT & BUTLER'S CIG

SYDNEY KYTE

LAMBERT & BUTLER'S CIGARETTES

JACK PAYNE

LAMBERT & BUTLER'S CIGARETTES

LOU PREAGER

LAMBERT & BUTLER'S CIGARETTES

HARRY ROY

LAMBERT & BUTLER'S CIG

DEBROY SOMERS

GERALDO

CARROLL GIBBONS

NAT GONELLA

HENRY HALL

BRIAN LAWRANCE

SYD. LIPTON

JOE LOSS

RAY NOBLE

LEW STONE

RUDY VALLEE

PAUL WHITEMAN

MAURICE WINNICK